Awaking Adventureland

A Novel

Stephanie Estrada

Theme Park Press
The Happiest Books on Earth
www.ThemeParkPress.com

Editor: Bob McLain
Layout: Artisanal Text

ISBN 978-1-68390-252-2
Printed in the United States of America

Theme Park Press | www.ThemeParkPress.com
Address queries to bob@themeparkpress.com

Awaking
Adventureland

Disney Terms

Backstage: Anything behind closed doors at the Disney resort is known as 'backstage'. This is ideally where cast members sign-in for work, lounge during breaks, and prepare any/all needed materials to get ready to make every day a memorable one for guests.

Blue IDs: Essentially just work ID's. Ours are blue.

Bounding/Disneybounding: The essence of dressing up within the theme and colors of a specific Disney character. If you haven't tried it before, I highly recommend you check out Pinterest and give it your best shot.

Bump Out/ Rotation: All the rides at the park require cast members to switch positions within a time period, and this is just that. It helps keep them on their toes and works intricately to allow everyone a break.

Deployed: Usually this comes in the form of a slip of paper from a manager notifying you that you've been selected to temporarily work at another location on property. Usually this only happens when there are festivals going on that need additional cast members or when maintenance on specific rides/ park locations is happening.

Disney Look: The strict aesthetical guideline cast members must follow when working for the Mouse. No tattoos showing, no obviously dyed hair, no overly done makeup, no unkept beards.

ER/Early Release of Shift: This is when a cast member gets their lucky wish come true by a manager and they're allowed off work early! Super uncommon during peak season but is not unheard of come off-season.

I clamp a hand over my mouth, but it's too late. Devin has already heard.

"You're going to get me fired!" I growl, pushing at his shoulder. Devin, contrarily, has always been easygoing and shows no sign of caring about my apparent state of annoyance.

"Nah, they like you too much to do that, Abby." He snorts.

"You're right," I quip, turning on my heel and circling around him. "So I'd start to worry if I were you." I note, breezing through the dimly lit hall and leaving him behind.

He guffaws behind me. "What's that supposed to mean?"

I shrug, my back to him. "Nothing!"

"Whatever...hey, wait. Are you going to make it to Thanksgiving dinner?"

I turn over my shoulder. "You mean Epcot? I always do." I wink, knowing that tonight, at least, will be promising.

Disney World at sunset has always been special to me; the thought of a productive day and time well-spent always brings me feelings of content, and that, truthfully, is what drove me to join this theme park circus in the first place. I'd spent my childhood dreaming of something larger, and upon my first visit to the Mouse at just seven years-old, I knew it was only a matter of time before I called this place home. Someway, somehow.

At twenty years-old, I made that dream a reality when I became a poorly paid College Program kid. Severely worked and away from home, I learned that while life at Disney isn't a piece of cake...the free entrance is *so* worth it, especially on days like today, when we can put that complimentary, well-earned entrance to great use.

When I'd first started my journey as a full-time cast member, having graduated from Disney Jr. as a CP, most of my roommates and old friends moved on to bigger and better things. Devin was one of the few that had chosen to stay and turn working for the company into a career, and it was only obvious that a friendship between us would work well after being neighbors for the past year. CP alumni have to stick together, after all.

Exiting the park now, my costume folded neatly in my purse and my fall-time dress on, I can't help but feel grateful for the

Our windshield the night it was hit by a cinder block

Brock in Israel filming Discovery Channel's Miracles of Jesus

Barbara (from Mexico) and me the weekend we met

Genesis in Ecuador with her parrot

A Party with a Purpose baby shower

Rosa and me before we went over the border to Mexico

The Mexican flag

*Brock and me with Bariela, our Compassion child
from the Dominican Republic*

If this book inspired you,
please purchase another one for a friend.

Please join us by:

1. Praying for us as we go.

2. Going with us as we go.

3. Giving so that we and others can go.

www.brockgill.com

life I have. Who gets to clock out of work and walk back into the Most Magical Place on Earth? I know I have it good, and the sky just reinforces that, the sun sparkling a bright orange and the surrounding layout shades of aqua, lilac, and peach tinging the atmosphere.

"All I'm saying is Disneyland has World of Color!"

"But we have *four* parks!"

I can recognize those voices in my sleep, as their talking in my slumber is usually, and unfortunately, the case.

"Girls, girls," I hop onto the Epcot transfer bus, basking in that satisfying feeling of sweet AC. "Disneyland *does* have Cars Land...but we also have Pandora. Tough call." I giggle, falling into a seat beside them.

Beth and Anaya have been my closest friends since we'd sat through Traditions, Disney's Kool-Aid drinking/training session as CP's, but while Bethany now works as a Guest Relations cast member, Anaya makes a fortune off showcasing her Disney adventures, and sometimes us, on Instagram. We're all a bit secretly jealous, but we can't complain because she does get plenty of free merchandise and is usually kind enough to share.

"You ready?" Beth asks now, nearly shaking in her bright blue dress and sparkling heels, an obvious ode to Cinderella herself, her features naturally made to match. "Happy Thanksgiving!"

Epcot is thriving with a momentous amount of people seeking to avoid cooking a feast on this year's holiday. Left and right, booth among booth is crowded, lines running longer than I've seen since summer. A quick stab of guilt forks me in the heart for the cast members working today, but is momentarily extinguished by the sight of friends, new and old alike, waiting for us outside of Biergarten, arguably the best restaurant in the park to get a bang-for-your-buck meal.

"You ready to dance some Polka?" Devin appears in the flesh with his roommate, Bryan, as we're led to our table.

On a cast member-style diet, daily meals usually only consist of one in which everyone stuffs their face to the best of their ability. Lucky for us, it's a holiday, so at least we can justify just how much we've saved room for tonight.

"This feels anti-American," I jest to the boys.

It's Thanksgiving."

"I'm sure there's bound to be some sort of turkey in this place," Bryan snorts before he leaves us to take a place between Anaya and Bethany.

Unspoken rules of CP entail keeping quiet when someone is so desperately after a romantic partner it is glaringly cringe worthy. Though we'd all graduated from nights spent hooking up with other broke Disney cast members, we all technically still are broke, and also cast members.

Bryan, a lifeguard at Blizzard Beach, is by far the most logical option for someone who's climbed the influencer ranks as much as Anaya, but is still not quite worthy. It is also notable that she still continues to deny the one time they hooked up at House of Blues, so, well, you know...it's probably not going anywhere. Anaya is too busy pining after the latest Danielle Nicole bag and Minnie ears. Can't blame her.

Just as I'm thinking this, Bethany stands, twirling her glittering blue skirt in hopes that Bryan will be able to put a finger on who she's bounding as. He seems to shrug and poorly guess she's channeling her inner Sleeping Beauty. Amateur mistake; he's missed the glass slipper necklace she's wearing.

And, see, this is where it gets fun.

Anyone with a set of eyes knows that Bethany has been dying for Bryan's attention since we'd walked through the casting doors on Day 1 of our Fall College Program. She's only ever said as much to me, but Anaya put it together pretty quick and Devin followed suit.

Bethany does not know about the Bryan x Anaya make-out solely because Anaya swears she can't remember a thing, but we all know it's really because she feels like a horrible person in the wake of it. In the three months following, Anaya has since made sure to feature Beth in all her live Instagram videos, on top of inviting her to all her park hangouts with other big-name small shoppers and bloggers.

If you think *that* sounds bad, then I can safely say you've been spared the brunt of DCP reality. Cheating scandals, underage drinking, and cat fights are just the icing on the cake. We were the good ones, or at least that's what we tell ourselves three years later.

"Is it just me or is this always painful to watch?" Devin takes my elbow and whispers in my ear. I roll my eyes.

"You're seeing it in a very different light than me...." I say, but as I watch Bethany toss her hair over her shoulder and take the seat next to Bryan, I feel a small pang in my gut.

"You don't know that," his eyes glimmer mischievously and I guffaw. Devin is always playing the borderline flirt, and for the better years that I've known him, he's never made it clear whether he breathes flirtation or is probing for some reaction from me.

"Guess not," I mumble, and it's the last thing I say before we're grabbing our plates and heading for the buffet. Rule number 1: food over everything.

"I haven't wanted to voice it yet, but I think it's time," an entertainment cast member clears his throat at the end of the table. Some of these guys truly let things get to their head, and by the tone of this one's voice, it isn't just a stereotype. They are prettier than us, and therefore think they are better than us. I'm not saying they're wrong, just that it's unfair.

"Who is he?" I mouth at Anaya, kicking her under the table.

"Josh, I think?" She mouths back with a shrug. By default, any and all friends of friends are invited to all social gatherings. As one might think, cast members typically get on pretty well and don't go too long without bridging the gap and becoming good friends.

"I'm heading back to Montana." He finishes, and the left end of the table goes wild, questioning why he'd do such a thing and how they'll possibly live without him. Yawn.

Beth and I exchange an eye roll that is met with a jab in the gut from Devin.

"Oh no!" he exclaims, loud enough for everyone to think he's suffering right along with them, and I let out an involuntary snort, knowing full well he has no idea who this Josh is and doesn't care if he heads back to Alaska.

Somewhere deep down? I feel bad. Losing a roommate or work bestie is like losing family. Most of us are living out a dream working here, but without our real families, most of us have made our own.

My folks? Up in West Palm. Far enough to not bother, but close enough if I need them. I never came here to run from my parents, but I have to say that this place is a more than decent escape location.

"I just think I need to get back to school and land a real job." Pretentious Josh remarks, metaphorically digging the nail in the coffin. How many eye rolls are too many? I've outdone myself.

"Yep, he's a dick." I whisper, and Devin is now the one who snorts along with everyone on the righter end of our table.

There is an undeniable sense of taboo around leaving Disney. There's no precise way to describe it, but there's a responsibility that comes with moving here for the Mouse. Full-timers don't take kindly to those that don't consider our jobs the "real deal," and it shows.

"And to think that everyone is so fooled by your little-miss-nice shenanigans." Anaya snickers.

"Eat your cheese soup, girl. Eat. Your. Soup."

As we continue to hear Josh discussing life outside of Orlando, I find myself immersed in his reasons for leaving: family, money, a career, travel.

I, like most of us, finished my schooling online and still have a bachelor's degree to my name, but can't help but feel a little sting at the thought of this not counting as a grown-up job.

What exactly would we call it, anyways?

Will most of us go on to leave and find better paying jobs? I'd bet on it, but I also don't think that time is anywhere near now. If given the choice, we'd all prefer to move up within the Disney ranks rather than leave to start somewhere new.

"I'm feeling less successful right about now," Anaya clucks her tongue and we all give her equal looks of disparity. If anyone here is part of the winner's circle, it's the girl who convinced Corbin Bleu to jump rope for her social media platform.

"Please," Bryan nudges her. "You've found your purpose, right? Your thing?"

"Mhm," she says over a mouthful, careful not to look at him for too long.

"Then that's that," he says, and I don't realize my mouth is gaped slightly open until the waiter comes along to ask if I'd like a refill of water.

"Nope, yeah, I need a beer. Sorry." I say unintelligibly, and while this is met with laughs at the table, I'm suddenly quiet.

Your purpose. *What is my purpose here at Disney?*

Everyone goes on eating their meals, and it isn't until I've chugged my beer whole that I formulate a logical, yet entertaining, sentence.

"How did we even do the program underage?" I say, winning a laugh from most of the table.

"Answering that in public may lead to my incarceration, so maybe it's better that I don't say anything." Bethany's eyes twinkle.

"Ahhh, yes. Who could forget the delinquent boys next door, hmm?"

Two

As a child, I always imagined I'd wind up a professor, only because I loved the element of reading so much. I like to think that the only downfall that comes with working at Disney is not being able to support the avid reader lifestyle I'd like to live. Fittingly, my degree is in literature, not that I have much to show for it.

Like Belle, for the most part of my days, I like to fill my head with books, only I do it on my lunch break. Today, though, the story I'm reading mirrors too much of yesterday's conversation of finding your way in life, and I find myself munching on a stray granola bar I found unclaimed earlier in the breakroom.

As of late, I've felt the strange sense that something is missing. Disney is quite possibly *it* for me, but I don't feel that I'm utilizing the most of my potential. Admittedly, I could be doing more than busting people trying to get up out of boat rides.

The lingering thought sitting my brain overshadows me as I head back for the exit at Pirates.

My partner at the unloading dock is someone I've never met before, and they seem as eager to speak to me as I am to them, so it remains fairly quiet as we let people through the line.

The rest of my shift, I rack my brain with thoughts of leaving Disney, moving to Paris, and possibly working for the, err, European Mouse.

"You know you don't have to wait for me," I nod at Devin as I clock out.

He's been off the job for about an hour now, but that doesn't stop him from waiting on me. He knows how sucky it is to be living in Orlando without a car, so in exchange for rides, I buy him the occasional gas or Mickey ice-cream bar. When I'll finally rack up enough cash to repair my own 1995 Corolla is beyond me.

"It's no trouble," he shrugs, pocketing his phone and stretching. "Now, let's *go.*"

"Don't rush me, I just got here!" I huff, but he's already speed walking. "You're so annoying." I grumble.

"Heard that," he says over his shoulder, and the rest of way to his car, we're quiet, switching between staring off into space and playing small games on our phones as we transfer from bus to bus.

Nobody likes to talk about commuting in Magic Kingdom, and that's probably because it's the worst. Waiting ten minutes for a bus to pick you up and take you to another backstage location underground, followed by another bus switch, some underground tunneling, and *then* walking to your car. It's a half-hour production if you've got the best of luck, and on a bad day, well over an hour.

I am happy here, I think to myself. *Maybe I'm just bored?*

I could ask Devin what he thinks...or he might laugh at me. Maybe better not.

The level of closeness Devin and I have achieved as of late is one of great comfort. It's scarce to come across true people you can trust without them wanting something from you in return, but Devin, I know, I can at least be honest with.

"So, I was–"

"I have an issue," I blurt, just as Devin lowers the radio to say something.

We exchange a quick look that questions which of us will speak first.

"Go ahead," he juts his chin at me.

"I feel weird." I state, fumbling with my hands in my lap. The five O'clock sun is brutal in my eyes, and I don't know if it's that or my emotions that make them sting.

"Did I say something?" His cheeks turn a shade pinker and I smirk.

"No, I just, yesterday's conversation made me feel icky, and I can't stop thinking about it." I admit, biting the inside of my cheek.

"The one about underage drinking."

"No, you clown, the one about leaving Orlando." Of course, I can't expect a serious response from him off the bat.

"You want to leave?" His usually casual tone takes on a considerate approach, his question betraying nothing he's thinking.

"No, I think I'm just...bored. I think I've just fallen into this norm and haven't thought of it much until yesterday." I hold my hands above my head and groan.

"Ahhh, I see. You're missing fulfillment." he muses. I process this, slowly nodding.

"Now that you say it like that, I think so." I squint. "Obviously I want to keep working for the company, but I also feel like there has to be something *else* besides clocking in and out of this place five days a week."

"Right, a change of scenery." He tilts his head to the side, peering at me through his peripherals. "Or a new boyfriend? A hobby? A vacation?"

"All of the above sound great but we both know the guys in Orlando are straight-up losers."

He gasps. "That is mildly insulting."

The possibility of a man on my arm or something new and exciting to take up my free time in a unique location fill my head. Grecian sunsets, A Brad Pitt lookalike, hiking through the Smokies, maybe developing a love for knitting?

"I could use a vacation, too, but we are all severely penniless." His hands drum the wheel, the gears in his mind turning. "Something completely different." We're quiet a few moments before he lifts a finger. "I've got it! Disneyland! Ha!" He throws his head back and I laugh, too, but then something hits me.

New state. New people. New places. A great escape.

"Wait a minute – Disneyland." I breathe, quietly. "Disneyland!"

His eyes grow large and questioning, unsure as to the direction I'm heading in. "How would we even make that happen?"

"I have my ways." I raise the stereo volume.

Three

"Is she crazy?" Bethany whispers to Anaya over her magazine, her glittering pink nails splayed across the glossy cover of *Vogue*.

After a day full of cleaning our apartment, we chose to reward ourselves with wine and pampering. Consequently, I figured it was the perfect time to announce the possibility of a small trip out to California.

"Not as much as you'd think," Anaya tilts her head to the side. "We'd only have to cover the plane tickets, and if we're lucky, I can find a sponsor for our hotel." Like most other notable Instagrammers, Anaya has her fair share of connections in the hotel industry that are more than willing to offer her a complimentary stay in exchange for some explicit word of mouth.

Another cast member perk? Free admission. To. All. Parks. Everywhere. Yes, all of them.

"All of us in one room?" I ask, the question playing in my head. Free sounds great, but where'd we all fit?

"Wait, who's even going?" Anaya considers her newly painted nails. She'd been debating whether wine red was the way to go, and I'd told her it might look campy. I think now she's seeing where I was coming from.

"Well, I told Devin." I shrug. "He was interested."

"Which means Bryan is definitely going." Beth drops her magazine. "We *have* to go, guys!"

"Oh, no," I groan before I can stop myself, Anaya's eyes meet mine with laser focus.

"What does that mean?" Beth drops her mag. Just as I presumed: Bryan is a sensitive topic.

"He's boring. You could do so much better." I reply absentmindedly. "Don't you think if something was going to happen it would have by now?" I raise my brows.

"*Well,*" Anaya clears her throat. "I'd argue that a slow budding romance is the best kind. Who's to say?" She smiles cattily and that seems to end her input.

"I guess," I shrug, but Bethany is quiet. I've upset her.

"I didn't mean to be rude, Beth. You're just so great. Maybe you'll find a California boy. Imagine the possibility! Romance, the Santa Monica Pier, Disneyland!" I squeal, and there's no denying that either of the girls aren't opposed.

"Whatever," she kicks me with her toes and I giggle.

"But I have a Fastpass," Ramona G practically wails.

You know Ramona. She is like every other con artist at Disney World, searching for any way to blame you for their problems in order to acquire some sort of goods. You know, the problems that they, undoubtedly, create themselves.

"Sorry, Ramona, it seems that no one in your party has a Fastpass." I reply, leveled and patient, assuming she'll cut her losses and carry on.

While most people at the parks are courteous beyond reason, there are always a few bad seeds. Said bad seeds have one sole purpose in life: to ruin yours. I can already tell I will not be going home in a pleasant mood.

Beth, as a Guest Relations cast member, has plenty more horror stories than I myself, but no worker at Disney is free of their own. There was, after all, that time I had a drink thrown at me at Food & Wine. We'll get to that story later, though.

"Sorry, ma'am." Jessica, today's friendly Dis-buddy, says, softening the blow.

"Ya'll should be sorry! I've paid thousands of dollars to bring my kids here, and I can't get my Fastpass taken care of?" Ramona nearly foams at the mouth, crossing her arms over her very obnoxious knockoff Disney brand shirt.

"You never made a Fastpass," I slip, instantaneously feeling my face grow hot. *Since when am I so bold?* I point down at our monitor. "It shows us right here your past activity, and nowhere does it say you made a Fastpass for this location, or any other, as a matter of fact." I am also a liar, it seems! I can't see that much, I swear! "We're going to have to ask you to get in the stand-by line. I apologize for the inconvenience." My shoulders are tightly held back. I don't realize I'm holding my breath until I start to see stars sprinkling my vision of this woman's blond toupee.

"You are a *horrible* cast member." She spits a bit this time as she directs her words solely at me. I try not to let it do much damage, but my breath feels ragged.

"Sorry, ma'am," Jessica repeats, even less helpful than me.

"You have *ruined* my vacation. Just *wait* until I find a manager. You are going to be sorry, *Abigail*." She scoffs at my nametag.

The blood in my veins has turned to lead. My head is heavy and all at once it feels like my arteries are clogged with slush. My mouth is open, but I'm not sure what to say. And then she's gone. And I can breathe. I can breathe. I can breathe.

Screw that lady.

"She freaking sucks," Jessica reaffirms.

My cheeks may as well be on fire as other guests come through the line and apologize to us on behalf of Ramona's behavior. But, maybe she's right.

Maybe, I am horrible. Just another day as your friendly cast member.

My costume is rough and grainy against my fingertips as I pin the burgundy fabric between my thumb and index finger. I've never considered the quality of my costume before, but now I find it oddly intriguing against the brutal afternoon sun.

Devin's car is aggressively humming in the background, serving as white noise to distract the tittering of my thoughts. I'm certain his car will only last another six months or so before I'm forced to figure out how I plan to repair mine.

Why do people feel the need to be such jerks? Did she talk to my manager? Am I going to get a reprimand? I wouldn't be dealing with this problem if I didn't work at a theme park.

I imagine multiple heads growing out of her neck as she continues to repeat, "You are the *worst* cast member." *I really should get to writing a tell-all story. It would be entertaining, in the least.*

"Are you okay?" Devin takes note of the level of quiet I'm exhibiting in his car. My eyes blink away the thoughts of unnatural guest/creature hybrids.

"Well, if you aren't the thirteenth person to ask me that!" I cackle madly, but my head is still throbbing from a mix of stress and lack of hydration.

"Seriously. Ramona G.?" Devin smirks, attempting to lighten the mood, confirming the fact that no set person at a work location can keep their mouths shut about any sort of drama.

"I hope she enjoys the rest of her *horrible* vacation." I wiggle my fingers theatrically and he snorts.

"What are you gonna do? Crazy people love Disney. Or, well, they love to hate it." He pats my hand apologetically. I discreetly wish I had the capability to let these sort of things slide right off my shoulders as I know he is able to.

I nod my head in agreeance.

"Ease up. It's still early. Want to head to a park or something? I think they're open late tonight."

"I don't know. I feel like I need a Disney break."

"I can't think of where you'll get one."

"My apartment is pretty sans-Disney. Want to head there?"

"Don't have anything better to do." He shrugs, and we turn onto I-4.

"You can't go wrong with a fried peanut butter and jelly sandwich." Devin flips the sandwich in a pan.

As a native of Texas, he swears by a very limited amount of food. Fried peanut butter and jelly makes the exclusive list.

"I'm not complaining." I pitch in from my spot on the couch. Devin's fried PB&J's are darn good, but I would never actually confess that to him. While I'll never complain about his company, I have to admit I am eager to soak in the quiet I've been gifted minus present roommates. It isn't often you find yourself alone in my apartment.

"Only because you're not cooking." He sing-songs back at me and I shrug unabashedly. He has a point.

"Thank you for being my pirate in raggedy armor. I'll get you a cronut next time we're at Epcot to call it even." I say over the sound of *Fixer Upper*. "I want a tiny house," I note in a whisper, envious of the home improvements Bill and Joanna Gaines are capable of.

"Tiny homes are pretty cool. You know, Austin is only a few hours from Waco." Devin drops down next to me, knocking into my shoulder, and hands over a plate. The steam of the sandwich mingling with the fruity, nutty scent is enough to drive my senses wild.

"Really," I quip, my fingers clamping onto the cinnamon sugar sprinkled crust. This, as he claims repetitively, is the secret to their grandeur quality.

"Yeah!" He repositions himself so that he's given me some space, but our shoulders are still touching on the small couch. "Maybe we can do a Texan road trip one of these days. Visit the ole' stomping grounds in Austin and I'll drive you to Waco."

"That sounds like fun," I smile at the mahogany floors of Joanna's current project. "I'd like to see the Alamo, too."

"It's a plan," he nods his head, and the sound of his teeth crunching into his sandwich gets me even more excited for my own.

Lifting it to my lips, I dig in and let out in involuntary moan when a sensation of flavor hits my tongue.

"It's amazing, right?" Devin turns to me, putting his sandwich down and rubbing his hands together conspiratorially.

"It's okay," I say, but it's through a mouthful that I'm hiding with my hand.

"Okay, I don't think so." Devin takes my plate and sets it down on the nearby coffee table. "Admit it: it's one of the best things you've ever tasted."

"Ehhhh," I giggle and put both hands over my mouth. He leans into me and rests his hands on my shoulders.

"Abby, this is dire." His eyes are green and large, staring into mine in a mock threat. "The entire existence as we know it relies on you accepting that this sandwich will change your life."

I loosen my hold on my mouth. "Can't do that." I usher the words quickly and his eyes narrow.

"Saving humanity comes at a sacrifice, it seems," he says, and then his hands are going for my wrists.

"That is unfair," I yelp, my voice muffled as he poorly attempts to move my hands away.

"Say it," he tilts his head to meet my eyes, and we can't help the laughter.

"No," I chuckle through a full mouth, shrugging like I'm all too sorry to not be able to give him what he wants. He puts my arms against his chest in distress.

"Come on, you're being a total Ramona!" He groans in annoyance and I let out a laugh so hard I can swear it makes no sound. My head falls into his chest as we both rock with laughter.

"Giving in that easily would be boring. Wouldn't you agree?" I peer at his face, squinting my eyes.

"You're playing with fire, Abby." Devin shakes his dark hair out around him, and I don't realize how close we've been until small wisps touch my face.

"Write me off as terrified," I lick my lips, grinning.

"If I didn't know you any better I'd guess you're hitting on me." Devin leans in toward me, but the scoff I produce comes out a second too late to be believable.

"Only in your dreams." I'm able to manage, if only to redeem my validity.

"*Only*?" His nose brushes mine, and for a moment there is an electric current flowing through my chest.

I should be saying something smart right now, but instead I feel my eyes drifting shut, closing against the heat of his skin.

Just as the front door swings open.

I gasp, jumping back from Devin in the most obvious fashion.

"I'm so hungry," I clear my throat, talking transparently loud and clear for whoever just came in.

"Oh, I bet you are," Devin whispers with a smile in his voice. I pick up my plate with a pulsating heat in my neck and face.

"PSA: We are going to California!" Anaya comes down the hall, yelling like they've officially announced the live action of *Moana*.

"What?" I stand, running over to her. "How? When?"

"Two weeks! We are out of here! Start booking flights!" She glides past me, hopping onto the couch and picking up my sandwich.

My eyes leave her for a moment to find Devin, and his face is so smug I could smack him. *Alright, we all know your sandwich is good.*

Now, if we could just explain what was going on before Anaya showed up.

* * *

"This sandwich could change lives," she speaks through a bite. "Let's go to Jellyrolls tonight to celebrate!"

"I work tomorrow," I say, my voice bordering on hoarse and confused.

"Screw work! We are busting out of here for a week, fools! We are going out tonight, period."

Devin stands, shrugging as he finishes up his sandwich and moves on to the kitchen.

"Hey, Abby," he calls and I peek past my shoulder, not confident enough to meet his eyes. "Mind if I shower here and have Bryan bring over my clothes? It'll save time."

"Oh, Beth will just love that." Anaya claps and I whip my head.

"What?"

"Bryan coming over. Bryan going out with us. Bryan coming to California with us."

"Right," I shake my head. "Yes."

"Yes?" Devin questions behind me.

"Sure."

Four

"Something weird happened today," I whisper to the girls as we get ready in Beth's room. Devin is showering while Bryan is in the living room watching *Jon Wick*. I'd die a slow, painful death if either overheard me.

"You can't possibly be talking about the fact that Anaya walked in on you two making out, can you?" Bethany interjects, slipping on a tight flowered number that has her looking like a 70's goddess.

"Anaya!" I growl, pushing at her shoulder. She lets me and falls back onto the mattress melodramatically. "Wait, we were *not* making out."

"We wouldn't patronize you if you were." Anaya sticks her tongue out and I grab a pillow to hide my face behind.

"Shut up!" I sigh before launching into a vivid explanation of what went on moments before she came in.

"You were flirting with him, Abby." Bethany's lips twist.

"And quite honestly, we're surprised it took so long for something like this to happen."

"What's that mean?" I mumble.

"Nothing except for the fact that you're the only one of us who hasn't gone out of her way to have fun with any sort of male in, oh, I don't know, *years*." Anaya fumbles.

"Okay, not fair." I idly mess with the hem of my comforter. Guys haven't exactly been on the brain. Making it here in Orlando, on the other hand, has. I guess the safest way to think of it is that it was something I never thought I had enough time for. Now, realistically speaking, it's not out of the cards.

"Just saying. Why not make out with him? Or, you know, date him? Get married? Have kids? He is *fine* in the most literal sense of the word." She reiterates casually.

"Hmmm. Maybe because I don't want to do any or all of the above?" I put a finger to my chin.

Both of their faces tell me they don't buy a word I'm saying. I may not exactly be against kissing him; he is attractive, after all...but we're friends, and I'm sure I'm okay with the kind of relationship we're lucky enough to share now.

"Want anything?" Devin looks over at me, the first real time we acknowledge each other's presence since this afternoon.

I scan the Ample Hills ice cream tubs and shrug.

"No, I'll hold off." I avoid looking at him straight on and instead pick at the dirt under my nails.

The shop is cold and I can't help but feel doubtful about my outfit of choice. The girls had sworn a nude bodycon dress contrasting my darker features was sure to win the attention of Devin and all the other guys at Jellyrolls, so I begrudgingly went along with it.

"You sure?" he asks me now.

"Yep," I smile small, crossing my arms before joining Bryan at the table where he's waiting alone.

"I can't believe we're going to California, man, it's gonna be awesome." His voice takes on a small southern drawl, one I've never cared for. Bryan is your simple kind of handsome, and it's no wonder Bethany's crush on him has never subsided, but I can say that what I've seen of him is enough to ward me off.

"Definitely," I nod, attesting. Bryan isn't a current fan favorite of mine, but I can't deny him that. "It'll be stellar." I chuckle under my breath.

"Beth's been shaking in her boots she's so excited." He hooks his thumb over his shoulder, and though his recognition of her existence catches me by surprise, I don't bat a lash.

"She isn't wearing any boots." I drone, and before he can respond, the rest of our passé has made their way back.

"What did you get?" I peer at Devin's selection.

"Played it safe. Chocolate Milk and Cookies." He scoops in.

I watch enviously as the three of them devour their flavors. When did I decide I wasn't hungry, again?

"Looks good." I bite my lip and see Anaya exchange a quick, knowing smirk with Devin.

I'm too busy waiting for her eyes to catch mine to notice Devin offer me his spoon.

"What?" I mouth at her, but she only juts her chin at him. "Huh? Oh!" I purse my lips.

He puts his palm on my back at just the same time. "Want?" In his other hand is the spoon.

"Don't judge me," I swipe it from him and steal the bowl. "This is pretty good." I nod, pointing into the chocolatey pot with my new spoon.

"Dinner of champs, huh?" Devin chuckles softly. I readjust myself, and he lets his hand fall away from me. I feel myself release a breath I hadn't thought I'd been holding. *What is going on?*

"Is now a good time to mention that your guy is looking good tonight? Hello!" Anaya tugs my hand, pulling me off to the side of the room where I hide behind a pillar.

"Stop it, will you?" I hiss, but she may know me better than myself.

Devin is wearing an opened Tommy Bahama top over a white tank and khakis, a full-on *Ace Ventura* look, but for him it works. There's something about a goofy ensemble that just turns out for him.

"Would it *kill* you to have some fun? You're so eager to want to change something up about your life, well, here it is! Enjoy yourself, even if it is just tonight." Anaya is pulling me out of my hiding spot, and I want to fight against her, but she's right.

I swear I'm missing something from my life...maybe, it's that part of me that's afraid to just say *yes.*

And as if on cue, Devin is there, watching me from the bar, and I have no choice but to walk.

"Pep talk me." I breathe, feet frozen, but my eyes don't leave him.

His eyes are sparkling over a clear drink, and I don't know what to make of the scenario. Devin has always been playful, but his look says more than that tonight.

"Abigail, you are hot. Devin is going to—"

"Are you *the* Anaya?" Someone bumps into us, obviously already drunk, and it looks like I'm on my own. There are few places where Anaya can escape her internet fame and I should have expected this is not one of them. Either way, we will find each other later. Bethany is nearby with Bryan. They'll keep an eye on each other.

I breathe. And then I walk, saddling up to the bar next to him, a questioning smile playing on my lips as I nab this drink from his right hand and take a swig.

"You continue to surprise me today." His lips are smiling but his eyes hold a few questions for me to answer.

"Do I?" I flick his chest, my confidence heightening. Glancing up, I find his eyes watching me, stealing whatever nerve it is I thought I had. "You know, I thought I was gutsy, I did. I'm not. Listen to me, carefully."

"What did you do?" His hand runs over his face, but he's laughing.

"Anaya and Beth thought we were making out on the couch earlier today." I admit with hooded eyes. Did I forget to mention I've already done a tad bit of drinking? I'd sworn it off after my College Program nights, but it isn't working out very well for me, apparently.

"Were we?" He moves closer to me so I have to lift my head to see his face.

"We were not. I told them as such. But...they think that I don't have enough fun, that maybe I should loosen up. I don't know." Jitters swirl in my tummy.

"If you came here to tell me you like me, you should have just said so." He winks, but his sure expression has slowly morphed as he raises his drink to his lips.

"Wrong again, Skywalker. They think we should, you know, actually make out. For fun. Or not for fun?" I raise my voice like a question, testing his reaction.

"And what do you think?" His tone tinges with curiosity and I am left feeling even more uncertain.

"That maybe they're right. I don't have enough fun. But I don't like you. I don't want to spoil this friendship. It's a dumb idea, right?"

He opens his mouth to speak but thinks better of it. "They're watching us." His eyes dart to the other side of the room and then back to me.

"Don't worry about them." I tug his sleeve. The prospect of something unexpected is actually pretty thrilling.

"Would you like to give them what they want?" His face turns childishly devious and while Devin is always a flirty, laidback kind of dude, this is a side of him I haven't yet seen.

"It would only be one kiss." I note with a pointed finger.

"I can't promise you won't want to kiss me again, but sure." His shrug is non-committal.

"Okay, fine, a few, for authenticity. Just tonight. This changes nothing." I wave my hands as though it makes no difference, but I can feel in the way my heart is speeding that it does.

"Don't want it to." He says and my blood flow comes to a halt. How exactly should I respond to that? And why am I bit disappointed?

"Well, that's surprising." I slip, not thinking to censor myself.

"What's that supposed to mean?" He tips his cup at me.

"A lot," I shrug, and he's shaking his head at me again. The bar is lining up with people, so he moves behind me to let others make their way to the front.

The place is full of CP's looking for a late-night hook-up, and I can't help but reminiscence. I've always been modest, though, and so most of my adventures were lived through vicariously. It's easier to egg your friends on than to do the deed yourself.

"Well, are you going to do it?" I ask over my shoulder.

He moves in close. "I have to make it believable. Relax. Get yourself a drink. We'll just talk for a few minutes."

"Okay," I lean into the bar, feeling his body close behind mine, a mix of nerves and excitement traveling up my spine. For someone who is so sworn against dating the guy, I sure am having an interesting reaction.

From behind me, he helps me skim the menu and lets me know that he thinks I'll like a Moscow Mule better.

"You think?" I tilt my head, and he presses against my back so that he can point out the ingredients.

"Yeah, it's pretty different. You'll like it, I think." He says, flagging down the bartender. We order and wait a few moments in silence until he brings back my libation in a copper mug. Aesthetically, at least, Devin is on point.

"It is tasty," I nod, slurping down through my straw.

"I'm glad you like it," he takes the mug from my hand and sets it down on the bar. "You look beautiful tonight." He turns me by the waist so that I'm facing him and part of me is too entranced to check if the girls are still watching.

"You don't have to sweet talk me, Dev," I roll my eyes, but I also feel a bit like I'm floating. My hands naturally find their way to his shoulders.

"Who said that's what I was doing?" He pulls me closer.

"Please," I pat his back and he laughs deeply.

"You were most definitely flirting with me today." He lifts my chin and my mouth gapes open. His expression is hard to make out against the darkness and the thoughts in my head are swimming too loudly next to the music playing throughout the bar.

"You are mistaken." I breathe.

"Ah, but I am not, Abigail." And he is closer. Closer. Closer.

"Why on earth would I waste my time flirting with a boy whose only talent is making women—"

Before I can finish, his lips are on mine. Time has stopped. Beer is socializing with vodka and our mouths are connected as if there is nothing that could possibly separate them. He is soft, gentle at first, and then, as I open my mouth, his kisses become more urgent, and his hands on me stroke their way up and down my back.

Devin does a wonderful job of distracting me from the fact that I am kissing someone who is too good of a friend to ever consider as a viable partner.

My heart hammers in my chest and everything from my toes to my head is thrumming with electricity. I push back for a moment only so that I can catch my breath, my hand on his chest feeling that he is just as surprised as I am.

"I can't breathe," We laugh together, his forehead against mine.

"So, am I talented or what?" he kisses me again, quickly, before backing away.

"As if I'd ever tell you that you were," I manage to say between deep breathing.

"That," he grabs my face and pulls me up to him. "Is answer enough."

And then his mouth is there again, hot and wanting against mine. We continue like that for a few more minutes, and I hate to admit that when he pulls away this time, I am more disappointed than I ever thought I could possibly be.

"Where are you going?" I ask playfully and his eyebrows raise confidently.

"If we keep going like that we'll have severe brachial damage. Besides, I think the girls got what they wanted." Devin turns, propping himself up against the bar and slugging an arm around my shoulder.

As predicted, the girls are watching us with satisfied looks. Even Bryan appears a little impressed.

"Hmmm, I'm not sure they got their fill yet." I lean up on my tiptoes and plant a few more kisses on his lips, knowing full well these will be the last, or at least telling myself so.

I simply hold his hand after. He grips my fingers tight and whispers close to my ear. "This changes nothing. Promise."

Right. I think. *Nothing. Nothing at all.*

Five

"So, you and *Devin*?" Ever the creep, Pirate James interjects from the loading dock.

"One, guests can hear you." I smile, waving by two guests to take up the third row of the boat. "Two, absolutely incorrect. It was a one-time thing. You can stop talking about it now." I resist the urge to roll my eyes. Facial expressions have never been my strong suit, and to say I did not once rack up a few points for accidentally rolling my eyes at a guest would be a lie.

I glance up at the tower position, where Devin is steadily maintaining control of the entire ride.

Working in the Tower is by far the toughest position, as you basically man the entire ride and everyone's safety. You glare at screens showing all areas of the ride and you make the calls. Someone is in the water? Someone's standing in the boat? Emergency stop needed? All the responsibility of the man (or woman) in the Tower. Minimal distractions are necessary, and while on most rides you can see said individual in this position, they can't look anywhere but at the monitors. Yes, that's right. Quit waving at them.

Consequently, it is a great way to get a look at Devin without his eyes on me.

A jokester at heart, his tongue slips just past his lips as he focuses on the task at hand. At work, you would never think Devin has the roguish sort of personality I know him to truly have, but most of you would also not know that the cast member before you has probably hooked up with Hercules or puked their brains out at House of Blues.

"Have you looked at Anaya's page? People are asking about it everywhere." James continues in between loading guests onto the boats.

My hands fist at their sides. "It doesn't matter. We're friends. It happens."

With Anaya's apparent celebrity status as a Disney elite, it has naturally come to light that the internet not only wants to know everything about her, but also everyone she is friends with. Beth and I have been featured on her page and stories plenty of times, so it's predictable that might happen. What I can't explain is the apparent fascination in who I'm dating and just what I do when Anaya isn't there. It might serve me well if I cared enough to create a platform of my own, but none of that truly interests me.

And, well, I'm sure you guessed that on that eventful night, certain individuals happened to be in the right place and before we'd made it home, people were posting and reposting images and videos of Devin and I by the bar. Anaya advised it was better I didn't look but assured me everyone was very excited for me in a very unnatural, disturbing way.

It's been a week since then, and while I can't wait to head out to California, I also can't help but wonder just how this will change things for Devin and I.

"Disney hook-up culture is so intriguing." James breathes deeply and I resist the urge to gag. If at all, the only benefit of kissing Devin comes from the assurance that James will most likely prey on other girls that are not me for some time.

Later in the breakroom, thoughts of what people on the internet are saying and just what they saw fills my head with curiosity, and before I can tell myself I will regret it, I am searching Anaya's page.

She is tagged in images with my hand on Devin's shoulder and videos of us laughing next to one another moments before we kiss. To be blunt, the entirety of the night was recorded for all of Anaya's fan base to see. People are asking if I'm still single, who Devin is, if this is the boyfriend I've been hiding. Few people are asking if this is what Disney influencers do on their off-time – the answer is yes, sorry – and the rest are commenting daily on Anaya's profile wondering when she's going to address the rumors.

A mix of emotions swarm my gut, from the dropping of my heart when I see images of us kissing, to the heat in my head when I read people's comments on how ill-suited my features are in contrast to that of Devin and vice versa.

"Whatcha looking at?" The man of the hour scoots into the booth next to me and I hurriedly shut off my phone before he can see. Instinctively, I glance around the room to ensure that no one is listening in on our conversation. At this point, anyone who is anyone has heard of what happened between us and I only want to avoid adding fuel to the fire. James is right: Disney hook-up culture is weird.

"Nothing," I say, once I decide that my mouth hanging open is not an applicable answer.

He bites into a donut and nods at me, his right leg jumping under the table. "Not eating,"

"I'm," I smile, trying to act the part of an unperturbed friend. "I'm not hungry." The words out of my mouth feel slow, stupid.

This is how it has been for the last few days, Devin asking questions and me answering in small bursts of dialogue. It's driving me mad in the worst way. If I wasn't absolutely mortified, I'd thank him for handling it so gracefully.

"Here," he hands the donut over and it feels heavy in my palm. His hair is slicked across his face from the sweat he's produced during his stressful shift up in the Tower. "You have to eat something or this shift will kill you."

"Thanks," I break off a small bite, ignoring the fact that his mouth has just been on the same donut.

"We're going to Hollywood tonight, you coming?" He swipes the donut back and continues to munch on his quick lunch.

"I didn't know you were going," I purse my lips, ignoring the small frog that has permanently lodged itself in my throat.

"Do you not want me there?" Devin makes the question out to be lighthearted, but there is a moment where his leg stops moving, so I know I've surprised him.

"No, no," I flick my wrist. "Silly, I just didn't know. Now I know I'll enjoy myself."

"Good," his smile is wide and bright. For the first time in a week, things feel normal. I'm thankful to have that back, but one thing is certain: I am paying much more attention to this man than I ever have.

I should have never kissed Devin.

* * *

"I thought it would just be girls." I cross my arms, chin pointed at Beth. It's hard to make out the most of her face in the darkness, but the red lights on her Star Wars ears make it a bit easier. Anaya and the rest of her Instagrammer gal pals are behind us, snapping photos upon photos of their latest get-up.

She shrugs, a rueful smile on her face "I invited Bryan... Bryan invited—"

"Devin!" I clear my throat and announce theatrically, running to him. "We've been waiting for you."

"We?" Devin bows his head doubtfully.

"No one else will come get a turkey leg with me. I need you." I glance back at Beth, my eyes deathly.

"Is that so?" he swings an arm across my shoulder, turning me in the direction of the turkey leg cart. I can feel the way the rest of our group stops, studying the way we interact, speculating what will happen next. I'm less concerned about being photographed here at the park in the dark, but I know the possibility still stands.

"Certainly, "I smile up at him, thankful to find a reason to avoid having to converse with Anaya's friends for another minute. Don't get me wrong, they're sweet, but our priorities aren't exactly aligned.

At the counter, I pay for Devin's food as a thank you for multiple favors that I refuse to address, and he kindly reminds me he'll catch the tab next time. We sit on a mall bench nearby with prime view of the currently out-of-commission Chinese Theatre.

"I like your ears," he taps my skull after a while of silence, once our turkey legs have mostly been consumed.

"Thanks," I absently fix the headband. "They're from some small shop that sent them over to Anaya to test out. Cool, right?" I mentally pat myself on the back for being able to say more than I previously had today.

"Yeah," he nods, and his eyes flit around my head. I take the moment to appreciate the tan of his skin, the set of his cheekbones.

"Maybe we should start our own Instagram page," I wink, and when he grins I feel a sense of hope.

"Do we have an audience to please?" His leg bumps mine but he makes no move to draw it away.

"Truthfully? We might." I turn so that my arm falls behind the bench and I can see him full-on. He snorts. I shake my head. "So, you know?" I meet his eyes hesitantly. The now-familiar sparkle in his eye from the other night is there.

"Of course, I've seen all of it. What can I say? We're beautiful people and the world wants what it wants." His stretches his arms out wide graciously.

"I bet," I bring my legs to my chest, resting my head on my knees.

"Doesn't matter, though. Everyone will forget about it soon enough." He tilts his head at me like we have nothing to worry about, but he is way, way off.

"Do you regret it?" I look down at my shoes, damning myself for even voicing the question. I can't look at him, in fear of any reaction he might give. I'm not sure though which response it is that might disappoint me.

"Do you?" His voice is just as uncertain. The sounds of Anaya's friends laughing around us tell me that our group is getting ready to move, and I feel my patience wan thin.

"Should I?" I breathe the words out, afraid to show any sort of consistency that might give away how much I've been thinking about our kiss.

"I don't see why you should. We're still friends. Nothing has changed." His reassurance affirms the fact that what happened that night was nothing and I'm mentally taking it out of proportions.

"Exactly. Nothing." I stand, offering up my hand.

I really, *really*, shouldn't have kissed Devin.

Six

Cast members work their tails off day in and day out. We deal with screaming guests, crying children, the works, but when our shift ends, unlike most reasonable Americans, we have fun. Point being, we can't say no.

Peer pressure is prevalent in the world of Disney and it shows. After all, here I am watching Happily Ever After from the top of the Contemporary resort. We could be packing for tomorrow's early morning flight, we could be sleeping. Instead, we're out in our best garb with no plan of slowing down.

I'll never understand how a full load of work can't keep us from partying once the day should be dead and done.

My current theory is that there is a sense of finite that comes with working for this company. Nothing is certain. Friends come and go, roommates leave, neighbors get let go, people grow up. You never know when it'll be your last chance to just enjoy yourself. So, we just do.

"To Cali!" We bump champagne glasses at California Grill as the fireworks come to a start. While friends who won't be joining us on our trip are here, everyone cheers in excitement for the adventure.

As the buzz dissipates, a silence overtakes the room as every single individual in the restaurant comes to a halt to watch the sky. No one, even us cast members, speak for some time.

"Why is it just as awesome the hundredth time as it was the first?" Bethany sighs dreamily, and even though I'm convinced she's talking to Bryan, I pitch in my two cents.

"Magic is magic," I sip slowly, relishing in the pinks and blues that light up the sky before me.

Wherever I end up in life, I can rest easy knowing if it isn't here, it won't hold a candle to the life I have now. Disney will always be peak for me, and that, if anything, confirms that I won't be going anywhere, at least not willingly for some time. I have found my place among these misfits.

Anaya's phone is out, per usual, and she makes sure to grab us all in her screenshot. "Say hi, everyone!" she bellows and we all give an obligatory wave. A few moments later, she waves the camera around again before stopping on me. "Abigail, you are looking like a total Daisy in that dress! Can you repeat what you just said in a circa 1920's voice."

"Is there such thing as that?" I snort, holding out my champagne glass, regardless. "Magic is magic, darling!" The table erupts in fits of laughter and everyone repeats my words in equally gregarious tones.

"If she's talking *Great Gatsby*, she does know it doesn't end that well for her, right?" Devin takes up the unoccupied seat next to me. I shrug.

"She is, and she might."

"Do you see this, people? I am right here! I can hear you!" Anaya mock-yells as I take notice that the camera is on us. Per unnecessary Instagram manual, anything posted online must be melodramatic. I don't know what it is exactly, but I did have Anaya explain it to me once. Followers just respond better to high-pitched voices.

"Anaya, dearest, you know we aren't allowed to be seen together in public online anymore," I put a tired hand to my forehead and Devin contains his laughter next to me.

"I can't handle the fame," Devin chimes in.

"Why, it will absolutely kill him." I cluck my tongue, knowing we are intentionally ruining any viewership Anaya has established.

"Precisely, old sport!" He lifts a finger and Anaya hurriedly takes the camera off us with an eye roll.

"Wow," I crane my neck. "That was quite in character of you." A small laugh escapes me.

"That's what I was going for." Devin bows in his seat and I pat his shoulder lightly.

"Hats off to you, I've met my match." The words come out the way they always do when my friends convince me to leave my apartment and let me drink.

"You ain't seen nothing yet." Devin clears his throat and we watch the rest of the fireworks in silence, aware that almost everyone else is still entranced. A moment within a moment. Now, how, exactly, will I manage spending every waking moment of the next week in Devin's presence without betraying my emotional mayhem?

Seven

"I am not worthy," I breathe, taking in the Egyptian cotton sheets and the plethora of complimentary snacks that line the bed. "I. am. Not. Worthy."

"No, we are not." Devin rubs his hands behind me hungrily. Before we can take a single step forward, Anaya is in our way.

"Correct, no one is worthy. That is why when I ask you to help me with a photoshoot this week, all of you, and I mean everyone, is going to help." She points back and forth between the both of us and we nod enthusiastically.

"Yes, sure," I snicker, momentarily lodging the thought far away from my present state. Expectedly, we'll have to contribute somehow. I just don't want to think about it at the moment.

"Definitely, yes," Bethany pushes past her and flies onto the mattress. "Free! How is it all free!" She chuckles in delight and I plop onto the mattress behind her.

"Easy," Bryan occupies himself with glancing through all the complimentary vouchers we've been given. To anyone else, discounts look like discounts, but to us, in a five-star hotel suite, it just means we have another job to do: visit said places and pump out some content for readers to digest online.

"She's sold her dignity for it." I cut him off, sending a wink Anaya's way, but she is feeling less than jubilant. Truthfully, the rest of us will most likely get to enjoy the majority of the trip, while she will almost entirely see it as work. I can't say I feel too bad for her, though.

"Just like I'll be selling yours later this week." Anaya runs a predatory hand along my shoulder and I shudder, knowing I'm in trouble.

"What?" I deadpan.

"Nothing."

"You're screwed, Abby. Welcome to the dark side, there's no way back. See you never." Devin waves his hand frantically in front of me. I shove it away but he's still shaking with artificial fear.

"Shut up," I smirk, but he's already walked away with a Honey Bun at hand.

"Bless our main gates," I sigh contently, my complimentary cast member pass seamlessly granting me access to Disneyland. The ding my royal blue pass makes at the turnstile is the most satisfying sound.

"Rub it in, why don't you," Anaya grumbles behind us as we all trek through the entrance giddily. Everyone forgets to mention that the moment you stop working for the mouse, he forgets about you. No discounts. No entrances. No perks. It's as if you've never existed. It's the nastiest kind of breakup.

"Have you seen this castle?" Devin whispers to me, blocking my view from the parks.

"No," I squint up at him, the California sun a worthy competitor of its sister, Florida's.

"Fantastic," he throws his hands over my eyes and stands behind me.

"Or do you mean...Fantasmic?" I snort under his grip, arms crossed. His chest presses up against my back as he slowly walks me forward.

"Wow, and I'm the loser? Alright, Abby." He chuckles deeply, but it's endearing.

With my vision stolen, I have no choice but to trust Devin's grip and his steps behind mine.

"I hate to ask, but is this really necessary?" I put my hands over his but he doesn't budge.

He leans close and whispers, "Just give me a second, kid." I sag against his grip then and let him continue to lead the way.

The sounds of laughter and excitement around me make me impatient. The smell of popcorn and ice cream meld into a glorious cacophony of theme park food.

I can't wait to see it all.

"Ready?" he asks, and when he does it's the happiest I've been all day.

"Yes!" I throw my hands up and his palms fall from my eyes.

"There it is!" he yells and there is a small tinge of laughter to his voice.

A medley of pink and blue, stony gray make up Sleeping Beauty's castle. It is graceful and elegant, grand and miraculous. Whereas Cinderella's castle is ashy and classic, grandeur and inspirational. It's...

"God, it's so small!" I double over in laughter, Devin holding me upright as my body sways to and fro.

"That's what she said," Bryan blurts and for once he manages to make us all laugh.

"I am so.... underwhelmed," I manage through fits of laughter. Devin is just as humored, and all he can do is shrug. "I think that I'm going to faint from how disappointed I am." I start to crumble as I fall. Devin picks me up just like the noble prince he is and I go limp in his arms.

Only the kind of friends I have would laugh.

"Cinderella's done for the night!" Anaya whistles as Bethany and Bryan cheer. I laugh through my teeth, still attempting at playing dead.

"You're so bad at that," Devin mumbles, setting me down quietly. I chuck his shoulder and he shakes his head. Only then do I realize I've been immortalized on Anaya's phone.

"Don't look so glib," Devin clucks his tongue. "You know nothing is sacred when she's around."

The rest of the day is full of eating new snacks, exciting rides, and doing the very best of Disney. While Anaya can't help but capture some moments on her phone, I'm thankful she has tried her best to keep today internet-free. We take things slow, only because we have a whole week to enjoy the entirety of Anaheim, and opt out of a fancy night on the town for enjoying libations and pizza in our suite. Once again, compliments of the hotel staff. Anaya is kind enough to only include herself in the photoshoot for that, sparing us the embarrassment.

She'd given me the trusty honor of taking photos for her up until I'd said, "Smile for me, darling!" The honor was then handed over to Bethany.

"Do you ever worry about your liver?" I squeeze onto the sofa next to Devin. His knee brushes mine and I hate to admit that it sparks a bit of adrenaline in me. I've been able to tone down whatever emotion it is I've been feeling for him since the kiss two weeks ago but I have done anything but forget about it. On the contrary, all I can think about is the green of his eyes, the stubble on his chin (not at all approved by Disney, but lucky for him he's got a week of freedom until it has to go), the shag of his hair. Anything I catch a glimpse of, I'm able to distract myself with for a questionable amount of time. "On my deathbed, I am certain I will blame the Disney College Program for destroying the most of mine." I raise my cheap pinot bottle at everyone and they in turn raise theirs.

"I worry about a lot more than just my liver," Devin says, taking the bottle from my hand and bringing it to his lips, which takes center stage of my mentally capacity for a bit. *Why do these things only happen to me?*

"I'm certain that you don't," I tilt my head, reaching for the bottle that he refuses to hand back.

"Wrong, I do." He has one hand pressed to my hip while he holds the bottle out of reach with the other. "I'd be careful, last time we got in a tussle it didn't end well."

"Says who," I hear Anaya mumble under her breath on my other side, but luckily I'm able to snatch the bottle from Devin's hand

I can't imagine what expression must be on my face, but everyone is quick to make eye contact and then promptly look away. With age, I always thought I'd grow out of my shy, timid persona. I was wrong. Here I am, quietly suffering in shy silence.

"So, what's the plan for tomorrow?" Devin allows me to take a swig from the bottle before stealing it away again.

"Uncertain, I'm cooking up something as we speak." Bethany taps away on her phone, smiling into the screen.

Eight

"We'll just sneak her in." Bethany shrugs a shoulder. Bryan nods behind her.

"Okay, I thought I was against this a minute ago. Now I am *really* against this." I sigh loud enough to sound like the prude I am. Devin's hand on my shoulder tells me it's alright, though. "If we get busted, we are so termed it is not even funny."

"Abby," Bryan coos, his Star Wars costume an onset sign I should not trust a single word that comes out of his mouth. "We work for the company...we have blue ID's...we're going to a cast member event. It's no problem." He stares me down and I suck in my lip, nodding.

When earlier today Bethany had mentioned sneaking into Galaxy's Edge tonight, I had nodded and assumed it was something on her mind but nothing we'd ever actually do. I didn't consider that Bethany is from California and still has a few connections here, or that we technically do have blue ID's (the equivalent of regular work ID's) and if we get away with it, it really will be a great thing.

Occasionally, Disney offers exclusive nights where the park shuts down early and there is complimentary food, music, and rides for their hard-working cast members. They're completely free to us all, but usually only for the cast members who work at that specific park. The obvious obstacle here is that we don't even work for the California branch. Now, it's being offered up for Galaxy's Edge, an impossible land to get to during regular hours, and while it sounds great, I am who I am.

"I'm trying to convince myself it'll be fine, but I'm not fine."

Would this be the worst thing I've done while working for Disney? No, far from it. But it is close enough up the list for me to not want to risk.

"Cool it," Anaya comes to wrap me in a hug. "It's not like we're sneaking into the Matterhorn basketball court."

She has a point, so I cave under peer pressure. When I follow everyone downstairs and into the van of Bethany's unknown friend, I do my best to not make a show of huffing and puffing.

Anaya never returned her Blue ID when she quit the company and still carries it everywhere. There is, of course, the problem that hers easily looks outdated if you pay any attention to it.

Which is why she is lying below my feet. Under a blanket.

From the looks of it, everyone is too excited about seeing Galaxy's Edge in all its glory to be worried themselves or notice that I'm clearly on edge.

Disney doesn't take kindly to people who try and pull a fast one over them, and even though I'm –

"I can hear you thinking, relax." Devin kicks my leg, which is followed by the sound of Anaya grunting below us. Her head is poking out from under the blanket in the dark, her fingers tapping away at nothing other than her cell phone.

"Can you admit that this is at least a horrible idea?" I grip the Chewbacca ears Anaya lent me for the night tightly in my hands.

"I rather not feed your doubts," Devin jokes, taking the ears from me and putting them off to the side. "We're going to have a nice time tonight."

"Mhm," I grumble.

Before we know it, we've pulled up to the entrance of the cast member parking lot where our ID's will be checked. Anaya, still as agile as she was back when we we're just College Program scoundrels, is dead silent and immobile under the sheet.

My leg is shaking more than I know it and Devin has to put a hand on my knee to stop me. "Hey, just pay attention to me. Calm down. You'll be the one to give us away," he whispers in my ear as Bethany's friend rolls down her window and greets the parking cast member.

"If I can have everyone's ID, please?" A tall, gangly man asks, flashing his light at each of us inside.

"Gee, thanks," I turn to Devin. He puts a hand under my chin.

"Distract yourself," he says low enough for no one in the car to hear but us.

"How should I do that?" I tilt my head in his grip and he gives me a half-smirk.

"How about I buy you some blue milk tonight?" He winks and I hold a straight face for about two seconds before I'm grinning.

"Whatever makes you happy," I bite my cheek just as the flashlight hits our faces again.

"Open the trunk, please." I hear at the front of the car, and while I can't feel her, I know Anaya has tensed.

"Sure," Bethany's friend answers joyfully. As I turn to make out the look on her face, Devin scoots closer and takes my face in both hands.

"I mean, it might." Devin clears his throat and my brain is split in two, distracted by the sound of his deep drawl and concerned with whether or not I'll have to check out some new job openings starting tomorrow.

"Might...might what?" I say as Devin rubs his thumb over my cheek.

He lifts a shoulder as the trunk opens behind our heads. It's too dark to make out the expression on his face, but small bits of light hit his eyes as the flashlight searches the end of the car.

"Buying you a drink." He lowers his head so that our eyes are level and I see the small glint of mischief in them again. "It might make me happy."

"Hmm. 'Might' is definitely not anything to fawn about." I play coy and the trunk shuts affirmatively behind us. I do my best to hold in a sigh of relief as Devin's grip doesn't waiver.

"What kind of reaction are you hoping for, then?" He chuckles under his breath and the sound of his laughter feels dangerous. We hold each other's gaze questioningly and with a rueful smile, I start to open my mouth, uncertain of just what will come out.

Just then, the car lurches forward and we are on our way.

Devin is still cradling me in his hands. I laugh, shaking my head. "I—"

I don't know, I almost want to say. *I haven't figured it out myself.*

When we're far enough away to go undetected, everyone cheers, including Anaya, who sits up and releases a deeply held breath as if she'd previously been forced into an air locked slumber.

"We did it," she whoops and I grab Devin's hands, moving them away from my face. "Yes!" I give them a quick squeeze. He squeezes back, but there's a palpable tension that's new.

"Astounding," I breathe, having ridden Smuggler's Run three times and fully capable of riding three more. The land is dazzling with sights and sounds I never could have anticipated. As a casual Star Wars fanatic, I'll admit I'm more than impressed. I am amazed. Those small contrasts from Walt Disney World's land are what make it distinctly great.

"Right? This is awesome." Bethany's friend, who I now know as Jenna, clasps her hands.

"Definitely. Thanks for bringing us." I say through my teeth, eager to hide the fact that I'm still the residential worrywart.

"Aren't you glad you took a risk?" Bethany winks at me and grin wildly despite myself.

"Unsure. I'm still waiting on someone to spot me a drink." I tilt my head at Devin, where he's lightsaber fighting with Bryan like the dweeb I know him to be.

"What?" He shouts back at us, his red saber clashing with Bryan's green. Bethany and I roll our eyes. She points her thumb back at him and I wordlessly shrug. Our unspoken language is a gift and we embrace it with laughter.

"Willing to bet he's jumped your bones by the end of this trip." Bethany whispers, shaking her shoulders suggestively.

"Who says I want that?" I elbow her stomach and she lets out a whooshing sound.

Just as she's about to damn me to hell, Anaya abandons her videotaping of the boys and swings her camera at us. "I know we can't post it, but we need to document this!" She shouts, her phone aggressively making clicking noises.

"At least get our good sides!" Jenna comes over, looping an arm around us.

It's a sweet relief to not feel the insistent pressure of having to look good for Anaya's online platform.

"Everyone, get in!" I call out and we group together to snap a shot at the party we shouldn't be at.

"Where to next?" Devin asks, leaving his lightsaber behind.

"Didn't you hear?" Anaya circles her arm around mine. "Abby's waiting for you to buy her a drink, dude."

"Oh," he says, scratching the back of his head and taking a step closer to me. "Yeah?" he smiles crookedly and something inside me loosens. I laugh.

"I mean, yeah," I snort. His smile burns even brighter under the glowing lights of Black Spire.

We head to Oga's Cantina, a likely choice for any Star Wars guru. At our table, we order an array of smoking lemonades, bubbling cocktails, and of course, blue milk. A large part of me is happy to be here in California with the group of friends who are like family to me, but another part of me is glum at the inability to be alone with Devin. Where was the shift coming from? And why am I only starting to feel like this now?

"Hey, English major, can you check this caption for me?" Anaya thrusts me her phone and I'm thankful for the momentary distraction.

I quickly scan over the image of us in front of the miniscule castle today and edit a bit of her wording, omitting unnecessary dialogue and adding a bit of oomph to encourage engagement on her post. "Here you go," I turn the phone towards her. "I'd tell you to hold off on all the extra exclamation points, but I figure that is a lost cause." I reach for my blue milk, crossing one arm over the other.

"That's the spirit," she titters with laughter. "Best editor ever. I'll have to start crediting you soon."

"Please don't," I sip from my cup, delighted by the unexpected taste of the concoction. The liquid is sweet on my tongue, with hints of citrus that give it a bold, pleasant flavor and a foam that numbs my lips and is a less enjoyable afterthought.

"Can you find the hidden Mickey?" Devin interrupts, but Anaya smiles and I know she's happy for the intrusion.

"Maybe," I lean closer so that I can follow his eyes. Maybe it's the extravagance of it all, but I can't see past the towering podiums and bar props lining the rusty walls. "Maybe not," I grimace.

"Everything about this place is so impressive," Devin's hands are clasped as he takes in his surroundings. "Look at that bar...do you remember the one on Mos Eisley? They took inspiration from it and just ran with it. I would love to see the engineering behind it all." He rests his head in his chin, eyes taking on a faraway look.

Though he doesn't mention it much, Devin is an engineer graduate. He's never said it aloud but I know his dream must be to work as an Imagineer for one of the parks.

"Maybe you could do some engineering here, yourself." I suggest, and while he keeps his head in his hands, he shifts so that he can see me head-on.

"I haven't told anyone, but I've actually applied for an interning position back home."

My stomach plummets and I feel speechless. Of course, Devin never planned to stay in Florida. It was my misstep to think that his plans were anywhere similar to my own.

"Texas." I deadpan, turning my head away in fear of my thoughts being read so easily from the look on my face.

"No, Orlando." He takes my hand and tugs. I glance up.

"Oh," I say slowly, releasing a breath and letting my heart slow. I shouldn't have been so disappointed and I shouldn't be so relieved now, but I think I may be finally coming to terms with all the emotions swarming inside me. "Good." I try to smile, but it feels weak after just having been toyed with.

"You can't possibly think I'd leave you to make your own PB and J's. That's a disaster waiting to happen." Devin tugs a bit more on my hand and I guffaw.

"I'm sure you think so." I raise my drink to my lips to mask my laughter.

"Don't worry, I won't ask you to declare my sandwiches as a delicacy again." Devin winks, laughing behind his cantina mug.

"Please don't, once was enough for me to get it." Anaya scoffs and I gape. Even Bethany swats her arm.

"Don't embarrass her." Beth hisses under her breath.

"You're one to talk, Anaya." I say before I can stop myself, and at this, everyone's eyes go to me. *Shit.*

The hand I hadn't even noticed was still lingering by Devin's drops away and comes up to grasp my cup nervously. I wait, my teeth grit.

"What's that supposed to mean?" Bethany looks questioningly between us but we hold each other's eyes, neither one brave enough to meet Bethany's stare. We wait another beat. No one moves. I sigh, breaking the glower.

"I don't know, it was the best thing I could come up with." I shrug and smile reassuringly, sending everyone into a fit of laughter. Anaya and I are the only ones who are quiet, and I know it is only a matter of time before she attempts to murder me.

"Thanks for this, Beth." I smile between her and Jenna, her ultra-cool Disney friend. "I know I'm a wuss, but I will say..." I pause, letting the momentum build. Everyone leans on the edge of their seats, even Anaya. "It was worth it." I groan. Everyone eats it up.

"Ayy!" Bethany claps. "I think we'll make a go-getter out of this one yet," she leans into Bryan, and while I'm not drinking, my brain feels all kinds of fuzzy. Devin's body close to mine. Anaya's guilt. Bethany's ignorance. I am nanoseconds from my head being ready to burst. And, of course, it is like he *hears* it.

"I'm gonna checkout the rest of this place. Want to come with?" He starts to stand, holding out his palm for me to take. Just as I start to reach for him, Anaya intercepts my hand, pulling me up from my seat.

"Come help me fix my hair," she says, and it isn't a question.

"Sorry," I mouth, but Devin's mouth is still quirked.

"Don't be," He nods. I smile over my shoulder.

Anaya wordlessly leads me to the intergalactic bathrooms, which are uncharacteristically plain, I must say, and is standing before the mirror, eyes burning holes in my skull as she reapplies lipstick.

"I'm sorry," sigh, wringing my hands. "That was out of line."

"It's fine," she shrugs, but her hands are jittery. "I feel tremendously guilty. I have to say something to her, Abby. I shouldn't have been quiet this long." Her eyes water. I'm stunned at her sudden brashness, but it mirrors the thoughts I'd been having since the incident itself happened. I saw it all, quietly assuming Bryan would be a speck in our time here in Orlando, but as time progressed, it became evidently clear Bethany had her sights set on him, and, well, anytime I brought it up, Anaya said she had no idea what I was talking about.

"Are you openly admitting that you hooked up with Bryan and know it?" I put a finger to my chin in attempt to lighten the mood. She sniffles and stands up straighter.

"Are you admitting that you wish you could hook up with Devin again?" Anaya counters, plastering a smile on her face.

"On the record? No." I cross my arms, faking like I'm actually thinking about it. "Off the record? Also no!" I glare, vaguely ashamed that she's accusing me of something that is hands down true. I might not know much of what else I'm feeling, but this is a distressing hard yes.

"Then, no, I am not admitting that I hooked up with Bryan and feel horrible about this." Anaya pinches my cheeks and offers up a lip gloss.

"You should tell her. It's not fair to her." I peer at her reflection, stopping with the head of the gloss inches from my mouth. "Or me."

Nine

"I would like for this one to do more than just take my photos," Bethany saunters up behind me in her 50's inspired Snow White look.

"And do what?" I once over Aaron, the photographer Anaya booked for our girls-exclusive photoshoot. He's average height, lean, and very abstract looking. He has the features of the sort of guy who wants to talk about contemporary literature and play you guitar till you fall asleep. Quite the dream for some. His blond hair is swept back under a beanie and his eyes are shaded by Ray Bans. I would argue he's trying too hard, but I don't have the heart to bother Bethany.

While we're a few weeks late of Dapper Day, Anaya insisted we do a vintage style shoot to commemorate the good ol' days. The boys took the chance to roam the parks and Downtown Disney District without our domineering personas.

Bethany's painted upper lip mole quivers. "Well, get my coffee, of course." She skips past me, brushing past Aaron to grab her coffee from the Starbucks counter.

"She's enjoying herself." I note to Anaya, a few feet behind me.

"I'm glad." Anaya hugs me in my Mary Poppins get-up from behind. I wasn't too enthusiastic about the color scheme, but you can't argue with Mary. Anaya went with Jasmine, because, you know, of course she did. She has to put her Indian features to good use.

"You girls ready?" Aaron approaches us with Bethany in tow, and we all nod enthusiastically, eager to please.

It's hard to walk around the park without drawing attention in lace umbrella's and stilettos, but no one has the nerve to approach us, though some do try to discreetly catch videos.

We learn that Aaron is an art student at UCLA and lives with his pet pit bull. We all but develop heart eyes for him as he snaps shots of us naturally touring the park as friends. It's great to be surrounded by my girls and not have to worry about the stress of work, and undeniably, my inconsistent feelings for Devin.

"You girls are naturals," Aaron laughs deeply as we pose along benches, enveloped in laughter.

"Okay," I grab the girls' hands and lean in close. "Which one of us do you think he wants?" We keel over in laughter, and at least we know the shots will be great.

"Want me to fix that?" I reach for Anaya's phone and she smirks over her lobster nachos.

"You read my mind," she sighs in relief. "You should look for an editing position. It would be a nice pay raise for you."

"And you'd have to deal with less people, big plus." Bethany slurps on her soda. Aaron is quiet beside her, casually checking on old shots and racking up new ones as we chow down.

"That actually sounds right up my alley." I nod, considering the pay bump and lack of Ramonas I'd have to deal with. If Devin lands his engineering position, it isn't like anything would be keeping me at Pirates, anyways.

"You know, sometimes I wonder why people put themselves through this. It's hot, people are whiny. It's kind of torturous." Aaron shrugs, his eyes downcast. Unfortunately for him, he is much too shy for my taste. We all glance at one another, wondering who will be the one to bite the bullet.

"I guess you're right, but I think, I don't know." Bethany is smiling at some far-off memory, or person, or place. I set the phone down softly.

"What?" Aaron lets out a small chuckle, almost as if it pains him, and my money is on Bethany being a sight for sore eyes.

"There's something magical about it." Anaya is the one to say it, despite not being a cast member anymore. "There's something about a place that can change someone's entire mindset, where people work for a fictional mouse that they look to for inspiration...and going there, with people you love? With people who love Disney just the way you do? There is nothing like it." Her eyes light up, and I know now that Anaya started her blog as an ode to her love to Disney but also as a way to stay close to it. Maybe even to us.

"Did we tell you she once drank the Kool-Aid?" I place a protective hand on her arm. "It's a one-time thing, but I'm pretty certain it lasts a lifetime."

"With that kind of talk, you should start a blog," Aaron muses. "It'll boost your content pay and really expand your platform."

"I've thought about it," Anaya shrugs bashfully.

"What? You so should!" I slug her and she smiles into her nachos. Anaya has found real love in them, and the Lamplight Lounge, understandably. They live up to all expectations.

"Only if you edit it, Abs!" Bethany chimes in across the table.

"Yes!" Anaya squeals.

"And let me guess, you'll put together the web formatting?" I rest my head in both hands.

"Sure!" Bethany is on board. It's nice to feel like a team, though Anaya and I both know there is still quite the wedge between us.

The rest of the day is spent walking far too much in shoes that cost more than they should. Luckily, the park is cool for December and it's a nice change from the Florida heat.

"Where do you see us all ten years from now?" Anaya prods, for once not playing with the camera of her phone.

"Are you *interviewing* us?" I ask tersely.

"Considering it." Anaya shrugs bashfully, pocketing it.

"Well, if you insist, then I'm going to say VP of the company. Dream big, you know?" I wink, knowing the chances are slim to none, but I can likely land a better paying desk job sometime before then that entails even better perks than what we're entitled to now.

"Working for the production studios," Bethany counteracts. We both let out interested sighs.

"Impressive, Bethany, impressive," Anaya nods, arms crossed over her golden lamp-shaped Danielle Nicole purse. "Because I'm sure you want to know, I think I'll have a Mom blog and a dog." Anaya purses her lips as Aaron rocks with laughter behind the lens.

"Will I be editing that, too?" I hold the heart-shaped Minnie lollipop to my lips.

"If I'm nice," she tsks.

"You guys are interesting, I'll give you that." Aaron's camera continues to furiously kick. I have had enough of the sound and am hoping I can make my exit rather soon.

"Are we almost done?" I wipe an arm across my sweaty head but Anaya grimaces.

"What do you consider done, exactly?" she laughs timidly, unpacking her backpack to reveal ears, body products, and above all else: More. Work.

"Not this," I grumble, falling into a cherry teacup in a heap of sadness. "We've had enough." I hook my arms behind the rim and hang my head, my sunglasses resting too high on my forehead to actually be 1950's chic.

"Grumpy is a good look for you." Bethany winks, joining me in the spinning cup.

Anaya watches us with a small, knowing smile on her face.

"Just a few more shots. We need to get portraits done with a few of the items and then we're free." Anaya hands me a small mound of bracelets and attaches a matching Mary Poppins brooch to my dress.

"Only if I get to keep my goods," I mutter under my breath and Anaya chucks my chin.

"You act like you don't already do that," she removes my limp form from the teacup and angles me closer to the actual ride a few feet away. "You can keep looking pouty, if you like it so much."

She's right. Anaya almost always lets us keep the complimentary pieces she has, and so we may not be financially compensated, but it's enough. We always have something new to wear, at least.

"Pouty is just her personality," Bethany sing-songs from the cup, her legs thrown across the spinning wheel.

"Hey," my brows draw together as I hold my hands gingerly in front of me. I didn't know hand-modeling would be part of the requirements today and I am sure I am not good at it. What I learned early on from Anaya's relentless tirades is that acting as normal as possible is what creates the best content.

"She's right," Anaya puts a hand on Aaron's shoulder, making way so she can see what his camera is capturing. "More to the left."

I move. *Click.*

"Now right, tilt your head."

I sigh, move. *Click. Click. Click.*

"I want to see your eyeshadow, look down."

I do as asked. *Click. Click.*

"Gorgeous, now smile." Anaya claps her hands together excitedly and I give it my best go.

"I prefer Aaron as a photographer. He doesn't ask anything of me!" I smile through gritted teeth, but Bethany is wagging her finger at me with satisfaction.

"You can do better than that," she looks at me, eyes on fire, silently telling me to do this right so we can bust out of here.

"Okay," I say, stretching my lips wider. Their three returning facial expressions tell me I'm not even close.

"No offense, but you look kind of pained," Aaron admits behind his lens and I mentally take note that he is not as great as I thought he was.

"Oh," Anaya suddenly slaps Bethany's arm repetitively. "Devin is coming!" she yell-whispers at me, urging me to.... well, I don't know. My stomach lurches.

"What? Where?" I'm instantaneously in action, straightening my spine, poising my feet, dropping a hand in my hair, and jutting out my chin in what I think is an attractive pose. My smile is meant to give no indication that I know he is coming. *Click. Click. Click.*

"Gotcha!" Anaya jumps triumphantly, fist pumping in the air. It takes a moment for her words to process, but when they do, my body tenses and then sags.

"I officially am over this." I throw my hands up in defeat, half-pleased that Aaron makes sure to capture that, too.

"Did you see that reaction?" Bethany bites her lip, grinning at the two others.

"The shock?" Anaya says.

"The loss of footing?" Bethany gasps.

"That smile!" Aaron admits, finally coming out from behind the camera.

"Whatever assumptions you all have are way off-base, I promise you." I walk towards them, my heels tragically scraping the warm cement as if wordlessly admitting my fib.

"Nothing you say can change my mind," Bethany holds her hands up victoriously. "You are so obviously into Devin."

My face is guarded, and while I may look calm and collected, I feel anything but that. I am silent, eyes flitting, awaiting whatever verdict it is they'll come to.

"It was the kiss," Anaya smirks, smug enough to admit that she was right to begin with.

"Oh, a kiss," Aaron becomes the most animated I've seen him yet, trying his hardest not to laugh. "Sounds serious."

"It's not," I assure him with a shake of my head, but he gives me a look that says he doesn't buy it. No one has in weeks. I can't blame him.

"Is that the problem, maybe?" Aaron ventures. A miniscule, nearly nonexistent, part of my brain clicks. Great. Fantastic.

"Uh," my brows furrow in confusion, but my mouth does not know how to form the proper words to explain my thoughts or concerns. "I..." I clear my throat, cheeks flushing a bright shade of red.

"You," Anaya grips my shoulders and shakes me. "Are so busted!" She throws her head back, cackling. Bethany stomps her heels joyously next to us.

"I can't believe it!" Bethany twirls around us. "Abigail has got it *bad*!"

"Oh, shut up," I drone, but my eyes are smiling, and I'm pretty sure my lips are too. "It's just a crush." I wave my hands noncommittally.

"Aha," Aaron says, taking my hand and leading us towards Mad Tea Party.

"If it was just a crush, you would have been over it, say, I don't know, two years ago?" Bethany tugs on a strand of my hair.

"Not true," I release a deep breath, internally despising myself for being this readable. I had assured myself that if no one else knew Devin was suddenly on my mind, my emotions would not be valid, or therefore, authentic. Now, they are out in the universe for anyone and everyone to enjoy, so I guess it makes it true. I have feelings for Devin.

"Just the fact that it took you this long to realize you have feelings for him? Hi, yes, Real Deal speaking here," Anaya chirps, eyes crossed. Everyone laughs, but I stand still with my arms crossed and cheeks squeezed between my teeth.

"Stop," I drone, but my voice is whiny and it only makes them laugh harder. We give the cast member our party number and Aaron waits off by the side as we load into our selected cup of choice. We go for the mint teacup for aesthetic purposes and he scrambles in behind us.

"Will you say it?" Bethany whispers so low I think I'm imagining it.

"What?" Anaya and I both lean forward, our elbows touching on the spinning wheel.

"Will you say it?" Bethany repeats. I roll my eyes.

"No!" I shriek just as the wheel unlocks and the teacup begins to spin.

"Come on!" Bethany encourages, spinning the wheel as fast as it can go while Aaron struggles to snap a few acceptable photos.

I lean back in my seat, a knowing grin on my face as I raise my hands above my head. "I refuse to navigate this vessel while I am being *harassed*."

"Wow, really?" Anaya giggles, her hair escaping its intricate hairdo and lashing me in the face.

"Is this why you saved this for last?" I ask next to her, my own hair coming undone. "We look insane," I bend over despite myself, snorting through my nose.

"Oh, wow," Aaron focuses on Bethany, whose hair is dead set on entering her mouth. We only laugh harder, plans of getting picturesque images out the window as we chortle like a pack of hyenas. The sounds of the camera clicking feel endless and I have reached an interesting level of delirium.

"We must look so unattractive right now!" Bethany tries to move the hair off her chin but it only makes it worse, now covering her eyes and nose.

"I can't breathe," I heave, covering my mouth to hide just how hard I'm snorting.

"I'm dying," Anaya's head is nearly on the wheel, which is what sends me off. I throw my head back and let out unabashed laughter that consumes me until way after the wheel has stopped.

"Guys, it's Devin," Bethany is still giggling but has managed to control herself enough to speak evenly.

"Yeah," I'm still a ruckus to be dealt with. "Okay. I'm done buying that one." I attempt to even my breathing, poorly, at that, and focus on the rise and fall of my chest, small bits of laughter still bubbling in my mouth.

"No, for real this time," Bethany says a little lower. Aaron and I both follow her gaze.

And there he is. Smiling, waving, and laughing, too. He is happy to see us, me, maybe, and I mirror the emotions.

"Hey," I mouth, raising a hand to acknowledge him. He mouths a greeting back and I feel my smile stretch wider. It only dawns on me in this moment that I am still recovering from a moment of lunacy and so I duck my head down quickly in attempt to fix my hair as we exit the ride.

"How embarrassing, I'm a disaster." I mumble, the girls and Aaron trailing behind me.

"I thought you didn't care?" I get shoved from behind and resist the urge to smack my teeth at the girls. The push sends me tripping over my feet, and of course, into the arms of Devin.

I look up at him apologetically but he only laughs. "Hey, looks like you guys had fun today." He rights me and I do my best to hide my shame.

"Oh, we did," Anaya purrs behind me. "Have you met our photographer, Aaron?" She puts a hand on Aaron's arm. "Aaron, this is Devin."

Devin moves me to the side so that he can shake Aaron's hand. "Hey, nice to meet you, man. I'm sure you've had your hands full with these three."

"Lucky for you, we were just finishing up." Aaron glances between the both of us knowingly, the hint of a smile in his eyes.

"Where's Bryan?" I ask, before the conversation makes room to take a dangerous turn.

"He went back to the hotel a few hours ago. I've been wandering." He shrugs.

"He's got the right idea, I'm ready to drop." Bethany hobbles along, slowly leading the way through the park.

I exchange an involuntary look with Anaya and know by the worry in her eyes that it won't be long before she spills the beans. Hopefully, she doesn't take the rest of us down with her. Though, technically, I am faultless, but not without blame. I'll deal with the repercussions when the time comes and can only hope it won't be catastrophic.

"I was thinking of grabbing a snack on the way back," Devin coerces me, taking me by the arm so that we inconspicuously veer away from the rest of the group.

"I could eat," I smile, holding my arms tight to my chest. While the California heat is soft and warm, the nights slowly creep on you until they cut right through you. As the sun slowly sets, I know the chill will only worsen.

"I have a few holiday coupons...popcorn?" Devin whips out one of the yearly coupon books cast members get as a consolation prize for earning less money than we deserve. Why complain about pay when we have free popcorn and fountain beverages for Christmas?

"Yeah, please," I say, feeling myself shutting down on Devin the way I did just a few weeks ago. Why was it that when I think of him romantically, I go silent? I was so used to telling him all my innermost thoughts that it's unnatural for me. "What did you do today?" I clear my throat, eager to stay far, far away from *those* thoughts.

"Went back to Galaxy's Edge, ate all the food. Jumped over to DCA, rode a few things. Kind of played it simple. Where'd you guys end up?" Devin exchanges his coupons for two popcorns and a soda at the counter and we wait, the smell of salt wafting around us as the crowd dies down.

"Where *didn't* we end up? We've been everywhere. My feet are killing me. It's a surprise I can even walk at this point. "I shuffle my feet as the cast member hands over our snacks.

"That's a shame, I thought we were going out tonight." Devin shrugs as we loop around and slowly make our way to the park exit. Anaya and Bethany are long gone. I wonder if they're riding their high horses, imagining Devin and I confessing our undying love to each other. Jokes on them.

"We are?" I ask, my voice dipping ever so slightly. "Going out tonight?" *Together?* I want to affirm, but I'm silent.

"Yeah," he takes his phone out of his pocket. "Didn't the girls mention hitting up Ballast Point? Check the group chat. Something about a service industry night, cast members only."

"Oh," I raise my brows, hashing up a bundle of popcorn in my hand. "Mhm," I mumble over my crunching, but Devin is too busy tapping away on his phone to notice. We walk the rest of the way in silence, the illumination of nightly shows and sounds taking up the taut space between us. It is quietly serene, but I can't help but feel like there is something I should be saying.

While I would never admit I fancy Disneyland over Disneyworld, DL does win when it comes to walking. Nowhere on WDW property can you venture from a park to hotel without wanting to scissor off the whole bottom portion of your body as an end result.

"I wonder if I should I change?" I ask smartly as Devin holds the lobby door open for me only a few minutes later when we reach the hotel.

"I think that—" Devin starts, his demeanor just as playful as mine, only to be interrupted (yet again) by Anaya. I'm beginning think she's made it a personal hobby of hers.

"Let's go, people!" She bumps shoulders with me as I step through the door, me on my way in, her on her way out. "We'll meet you there!" She calls over her shoulder, already making fast for the Downtown Disney District. The day I don't find her hot on her heels is the day I know something is wrong.

"You're lucky if I get there at all with these feet killing me." I sigh, breezing into the lobby and coming face to face with Bethany. "You clean up nicely." I wink and she glitters, arm looped through Bryan's. It isn't the first I've seen them this cozy, but it is happening more frequently.

"You already look great, but really, go get changed. We are getting smashed tonight!" She cheers, gone before I can ask any questions.

"Forgive me, liver, for I will soon sin." The elevator creaks beneath me as I whisper tersely.

"I'll just be a minute, if you wanted to wait." I tell Devin upstairs, kicking off my heels and pouring myself a glass of water. I didn't exactly bring anything to have a great time in, but I suppose there's something that'll do the trick for a bunch of disnerds looking for a good time.

"Sure," he says, walking to his room before thinking better of it. "Anaya, huh?" He watches me over his shoulder, hand on the doorknob, eyes downcast.

"Anaya, what?" I say, glass to my lips in question. The day has felt eternal and any patience I possess has left the building. There is a time for everything, but if Devin has decided that he would like to raise questions about our current relationship status, now is not his best bet whatsoever.

He lets his hand fall and pushes the other into his pocket. I want to say that I don't feel this, the invisible cord that binds us together, but I can sense it more than I ever have now. "She just keeps interrupting us, is all."

The look in his eyes give nothing away, and my only response is to drink, drink, drink. My neck itches as I chug, thoughts scrambling for something to latch onto. Where do I want this to go? Sure, Devin is maybe more attractive than I have ever given him credit for, and I happen to want to spend most of my waking moments with him, but what does that entail? How can I play this both cool and interested?

I tilt my head. "I didn't know she had something to interrupt." I say finally, simply matter-of-factly, and drop the glass on the counter before walking away.

The walk to Ballast Point is quieter, this time with no sense of comfort in it. My snide remark has driven some sort of invisible block between us. Did I think I was being cute? Was I trying to flirt? Jeez, I am bad at that. The girls will get a load out of this one.

I can't imagine what would make Disney think that offering a cast member night at a brewery is a good idea, but I won't complain about free food and alcohol, even if it means I'll need to deal with whatever I started between Devin and me.

At Ballast, the room is hazy but the crowd is lively. Guests line the bar, people trailing in and out in with drinks at hand. The venue is reminiscent of Baseline Taphouse at Hollywood Studios, but on a grander, less homely scale. Indie rock pumps out of the speakers, and while no one is dancing, there's too much swaying going on for me to believe there won't be a change in vibe by the end of the night.

"After you," Devin beckons upon opening the door, voice distinctly aloof. I cringe internally.

"Did you miss me?" Bethany pops out of nowhere, taking me by the elbow and steering me toward where our group has marked their territory. Devin and I awkwardly wave our greetings and everyone smiles tightly, eager to follow the latest in our rivaling drama. It's fine, I'll get my payback.

"Either you two just had the worst quickie, or something awful happened. Which?" She continues close to my ear.

"I want to say somewhat between the two but that would also be completely off base...Aaron, hi! You came." I say a bit louder in his direction. He nods sweetly before directing his attention back to Anaya, who's examining all the photos he's captured today.

"I dig the ambiance," I say casually, looking to Devin to gauge his reaction. He appears a bit less disinterested and hovers more on the edge of bored. Maybe, just maybe, I was a bit too crude. I'm aware that men have fragile egos, but I've got to say this is disappointing.

"Yeah, we need one of these." He's quick to look away, giving me a small chance to enjoy his features. He's strong, I've always known that, but his arms are larger than I've anticipated and his palms are rough with the blue collar work we're put up to on the daily. His cheeks are sculpted, narrow, and I momentarily long to reach out to him, apologize for whatever I might have said that irked him. His eyes, droopy and dejected, contrast his gleaming personality, frame the gruffness of his assets, and for only a second, almost nonexistent, I am stunned. Devin is extremely handsome and beyond that, a great man. He never hesitates to stand by my side or put his neck out for me. He is constantly seeking to please others without expecting any compensation and genuinely enjoys spending time with me. He is undoubtedly one of the best friends I've ever had. And I am a Grade A loser.

Rapidly now, the gears in my head are spinning and it makes absolute sense that I might like the idea of him. From the day he introduced himself as my neighbor on my porch, he's always been here for me. Hell, I can't imagine a future without him. I just never imagined the kind of intricate prospect I can envision now.

My actual infatuation of Devin would, of course, also explain why I haven't dated as of lately. Sure, I've had my fair share of options and infamous Disney flings, but nothing has quite stuck. And why should it, when I've always had the one-up right by my side?

I smile to myself at the thought. Of course, I've always had Devin here. Of course, it only makes sense that we just fit. Fit. Us. Together. I smile wider.

"If you keep looking at me like that I might just have to say something about it." Devin whips his head at me quickly enough that I have to blink a few times before I realize I've been caught ogling.

"How..." I start, shutting my eyes shamefully. I am an outright mess to be dealt with.

"Don't worry about that," he rests a hand on my shoulder and stands. "I'm going to start us a tab," he squeezes. I let my hand brush his before he goes..

"Damn, what is going on with you two?" Aaron raises a small glass with clear liquid in my direction and I shake my head conspiratorially.

"I don't even know," I laugh, smitten, and everyone joins in.

"The only thing I'm enjoying more than watching this unfold," Anaya climbs into Devin's chair. "Is these photos, just look at you!" A range of vibrant colors catches my attention on her phone as she sweeps through an extensive set of photos that capture the generic motion of emotions that encompass me through my daily experiences. I am indifferent, glum, tranquil, and finally, when Devin arrives, happy.

"These are amazing, Aaron. Sure you don't want to move to Florida?" I joke. It pays off to see yourself looking irrevocably you on film.

"This is too sweet," Anaya stops on the photo of me signaling Devin as he stands waiting for us at the Mad Tea Party. "You look so coy and he is just so happy. Also, honestly, how sexy is it that he just went and opened the tab for you? Abigail, you have him on lock, it is covetable." Anaya zooms in and out of the photo before flitting to the one of me melodramatically sweating in the prop teacup.

"We always do that, silly, and shush, he might hear you." I swat her arm, but between scanning photos she is too preoccupied to listen.

"Wait," my eyes flit up to Bryan. He is looking at me with an unreadable expression. I know he's overheard most of what's going on. "You, say nothing." I chide and leave it at that.

"Chicks," he says to Aaron, but good ol' Aaron is too meta to agree. He thinks chicks are cool, and that's because we are. If I was half as medaling at my friends, I would interject that Bethany should bring her attention to someone more like him.

"Everyone is in on it," Bethany says, leaning her head on my shoulder to better view the images. I disregard the remark.

"I've already sent a few of the photos to our sponsors, but which do you want me to post?" Anaya is showing me a pre-selected handful, but I am too busy leaning my head on top of Bethany's and wondering if I'm a bad friend by accomplice. It's not my place to step in and tell Bethany what happened between Bryan and Anaya due to my duty to the latter, but it is also my job to be honest to Bethany as her friend and make-shift sister. I don't want to be one-sided, but either way I lose, and right now it's safer to stand with Anaya, I think, though it isn't without culpability.

"Post them all, Abigail is Queeennnnnnnnnn," Bethany howls and I pull her closer, laughing.

"Girl, same," I say, glad to have these moments to share with my people. Regardless of where we end up in life, there are some bonds that can't be broken, and these are just a few of them. There is a sense of electric currents that radiate when we are together, and I've yet to find a feeling that tops that, though Devin is definitely making his way as a close second.

"Okay, realistically, I can only post a few, you know that! I'll forward you the rest to have fun with," Anaya rolls her eyes at our lesser-being request. How can we help ourselves, though? A small taste of stardom is never enough. "You know what, I'll pick myself," she huffs, thinking better of it, scrolling hurriedly with her ruby red Mickey inspired nails clicking away.

"I like the teacup one," a deep voice bellows behind us, stirring the air just slightly, and I feel the heat creeping up on me once more. It's one of those new things that I'm still deciding whether I enjoy or not.

Bethany clears her throat in an attempt at appearing unperturbed. "Which, exactly?" Her voice is a dead giveaway that she is fishing for something, but when I glance over my shoulder, Devin is nonchalantly holding our drinks and jutting his head at Anaya's phone like he's searching for the right paint to pick for his house.

"There, that one," he says. Anaya is grinning at her screen, the light illuminating her lips a bright orange. "Look at how much fun she's having, at that smile." He whistles and the heat grows. A force is pulling me, pushing me, begging me to turn around and see his face. When I do, there is the smallest trace of a smile, and then his eyes are on me, posing a question I've yet dared to ask.

"My hair is a mess in that photo," I lean my arms behind my chair, reaching for my drink in his hand, assuming it is the brightly colored one whereas his is obviously just beer. Our fingertips brush, but he doesn't release his hold on the strawberry scented liquid.

"And? You look beautiful." His words are brazen, unashamed, just laced with his honest, and quite possibly biased, opinion. Instinctually, I bite my lip. He seems to like the response I have to his words and his mouth quirks up at the sides, taunting me. I chew on the insides of my cheek as any sort of pride or condescending remark I had dies in my throat.

"Thanks," I say finally, hoarse and low. He pushes the drink past me and sets it down on the table, his face coming close enough for me to kiss, and then he's back standing up straight. The moment has passed. I want to sit there, meeting his eyes for a while so that my emotions can sort themselves and I can finally find the words to say, but that is neither socially acceptable nor the proper sort of response to this.

"So it's settled, Abigail is a babe and she needs to get—" Anaya does a little dance and Bethany chortles. Devin shakes his head. He's used to this, I remember. It's always been this way.

"Please do not!" I growl through my mortification, shoving her out from the chair. She is quick to relent, stepping aside so that Devin can take his seat back next to me.

"You should ignore them," I assure him, grasping the drink as a momentary distraction.

He laughs, his leg bumping mine under the table as he leans forward and puts his arm behind my seat. "I always do."

"Probably because the things you say are just ten times worse," I roll my eyes, leaning back so that the magnetic force field of his body can't pull me in. Too busy worrying about the proximity of our faces, my back makes contact with his arm, warm and solid behind my seat. How is it that something this man has been playing at for threesome years is only now starting to click?

"They are not," he chuckles again, a mix of confidence and bashful play on his part.

"You are basically a walking one-liner for any woman that crosses your path," I remark, eyeing the bit of beer foam that's been left on his lip.

"I think you have me mistaken for someone else," he shrugs nonchalantly. "I'm rather limited with the women that I grace with my one-liners."

"Are you? Why is that so hard to believe?" I kick his leg under the table, but he hooks his foot with mine and I'm left with our calves intertwined. My heart is racing and part of me is thrilled that he can emit this kind of reaction from me.

"Because I happen to like using them on you." He notes, once again taking on the tone of a man who knows what he wants and is well aware it's within reach.

I've always assumed Devin made a sport out of luring helpless women into his romantic clutches, but I'd also very seldom seen him make passes at any other woman...any other woman that wasn't me. From the start of our relationship, I'd come to terms with the fact that Devin and I were great friends, and he was just the kind of dude who enjoyed making spastic statements that could be misinterpreted as flirting. Wrong. I've been wrong.

"You have been doing that for quite a bit of time, yeah." I say, playing into this form of banter. In the past, it was always easier to ignore, but now, it's much too fun to pass up.

"Since the day I met you, you mean." He chides, raising his glass in cheers.

Had it really been this way from the beginning? Had he always harbored feelings for me? How could I have been this dense? And if I'd known much earlier? Where would we be now?

"That long?" I lean towards him, dropping a hand on his wrist. "Really?"

He rubs his thumb over my palm. "There's something you're not asking me, Abigail."

"Yeah, maybe," I grin into my drink, shaking from the thought of this, all of it, being out in the open.

"Let's go! Next stop, here we come!" Anaya leaps up, the rest of the group following suit. Devin takes my hand and pulls me up, the both of us knowingly laughing.

"I'm not *this* kind of dancer," I watch the steps of everyone at the Rumba Room, a larger Latin club with expensive bottle service.

Anaya has already swindled the bar owner into giving her a complimentary one, of course, with the promise that she will be promoting the hell out of it online. I told her I refused to be painted as an alcoholic and would help snap pictures but nothing else. She wasn't too happy about the latter.

"Like *that*," Bethany juts her head at the rows of men serenading girls with their overly excited hips. Orlando is a melting pot and I've been to plenty of my fair share of Latin bars, but between my friends and me, I was always the oddball out, much less cultured. Anaya was able to incorporate enough of her belly dancing into salsa to make it work, and Bethany is just naturally talented. They took all the gifts.

"I bet you wish you were now," Bethany clucks her tongue, and my eyes follow her own to find that Devin's been asked to dance.

"You've got me there," I watch as a beautiful blond plucks him from our complimentary unlimited bottle service table (ha!) and drags him onto the dance floor. She's quick to set the pace, something only a gentleman allows to happen, and then he's following along, slowly picking up until he's leading.

They swing, toss their shoulders, and spin until it's painful to watch. She claps her hands, shaking her hips like she was created for the purpose of choosing him as her dance partner.

"Wipe that look off your face, it's just a dance." Bethany pinches my elbow. I allow my facial muscles to relax, unaware that I'd tensed. I look away, grateful to have somewhere else to look thanks to the scheming skills of my friends. Anaya is quietly watching us from across the table, a small glass at hand, phone nowhere in sight.

I'm not sure what she ordered, but by the look of the jewel that's resting atop one of the corks, I'm certain whatever content Anaya is going to release will not get this place the attention the owner is hoping for. Sorry, but the truth is the truth. Disney influencers run things their way, and that's just what Anaya does. Call it business.

I smile reassuringly, but Anaya only lifts the glass to her lips. Glad to see I'm not the only one in a funk. As the song comes to a close, I snap my head back in the direction of Devin, where he's thanking his new friend for their dance and walking back to our table.

"Hey," he grins, a small film of sweat on his forehead.

"Have fun?" I do my best to smile but receive another pinch from Bethany which notifies me I have failed.

Devin is slow to tilt his head in my direction, his face reminding me that of the Cheshire Cat. "Didn't peg you for the jealous type,"

I'm stunned by this next level of admittance he's throwing at me and calculate my words carefully. "You know me better than that. So are you going to ask me to dance?"

The bob of his head is melodic as he reaches for me and I let him guide me to the dancefloor. I do my best to mimic what I saw earlier, lacing our hands together and dropping my other arm across his shoulders. I pray he doesn't feel how my hands are sweaty and shaking from the nerves.

"Are you a secret natural?" His right hand rests on my hip and he moves us side to side, back and forth.

"Far from it," I glance down, our bodies too close for me to look up. My heart is thrumming through my shirt and I know he can feel it.

"Hey," Devin unknots our fingers and puts his hand under my chin. "You have to look up at me." He raises my chin and I'm left looking into his eyes a mere inches from my own. "Feel the music, forget the footing."

"Um, okay," I nod and our noses brush. It's like an electric current flowing between us, so similar to the night we first kissed. "Am I doing okay?" I ask as he spins me, pinning me in front of him before whipping me back out and in.

"Truthfully, I haven't noticed," he slows us down, moves my feet between his and slides us. "I'm a bit distracted." I giggle in a way I didn't know I was capable of.

"This is hard," I breathe, going through the motions but looking around the room and seeing that I am far behind.

"So are most things at first," he says, unlacing our hands once more and dropping both his hands to my hips. I wrap my own around his shoulders and pull him closer. "What did you want to ask me, earlier?" He tips his head towards me and our noses brush again. My eyes flutter shut but my mouth feels glued.

"Who would have thought you have the capability to leave a girl speechless," I detonate the conversation just as Devin playfully dips me.

"You've been too busy ragging on my game to realize I had any," he rebukes and I giggle again.

"And what's your excuse?" I curl into him, the song ending. He steps away from me, let's me decide whether I'd like to move in closer or farther away. I want to run towards him but would only make a fool out of myself. I need to be careful with Devin. This isn't just some guy. This is *the* guy. I have to do this right.

He spreads his hands out wide, shoulders weighted. "Patience, Abby, patience."

I can do anything, then. I can ask why, I can tell him I have the capability to be patient, too. Instead, I open my mouth and close it. Repeat. For an English major, too often I have nothing to say if it isn't on paper.

He is swept up in a storm of our friends before I can find my sense of clarity, and when they beg him to join their pursuit of twerking to Pitbull, I watch them contently. There's a place for everything.

Ten

"Is this the Insta meet-up?" Someone taps me on the shoulder. I turn and am greeted by a cleat-wearing ginger in a dark teal t-shirt dress. I applaud her for her style, but the fact that she is chewing gum at Disneyland is making me want to call the Mickey police on her. There really is no such thing as a cast member off-duty.

Anaya has recruited us to help establish and run her DCA Meet-Up. We are expected to ride things, eat things, and enjoy things with all of Anaya's craziest Instagram followers. Great for her online persona, not great for my real persona. Disney has stripped me of my people person status.

"Sure is," I nod, the sunglasses on my face too beady for my own liking. I sip away at my Frappuccino, willing this day to be over. Meet-ups never fail to equate to drama that I have no interest in.

"You're Anaya's friend, Abigail, right?" Merida is asking now, squinting between Devin and me. Evidently, she is one of Anaya's super fans. She watches all her live stories and comments on all her posts. As such, she's been dragged into the production that ensued online when I puckered up and is now playing clueless to her own advantage.

"Oh my gosh, Anaya!" She loses interest quickly, brushing past me and running up to Anaya as if she actually knows someone she's only met through the internet. I laugh at my best friend's response. She plays the part too well, hugging her just the same and welcoming her to a great day spent with other Disney fashion lovers.

"Is it time for me to start making snide remarks about this?" I chew on my straw, watching Bethany and Bryan with similar expressions on their faces.

"Maybe," Bryan grunts, his beard moist with sweat. Did I mention he kind of repulses me? I have to disclose that to Bethany.

"No, not yet. Have patience, Padawan." Devin rocks on his heels, hands in pockets. While I got suckered into wearing the colors of Merryweather so that Bethany, Anaya, and I could make up the fairy trio from Sleeping Beauty, Devin got away with a Hawaiian style shirt featuring Baymax and cherry blossoms.

"Right, patience, that thing," I ponder, thoughts drifting back to a certain remark from just a night before.

"Mhmmmm," he bumps my shoulder, wordless in his response.

We spend the next hour waiting for girls to get their Starbucks and take photos to post online and hashtag *AnayasBigDayatDCA* with wound up smiles. Bethany spends most of her time distracted by Bryan's beard and little else, while Devin educates me on the bit of engineering that went into play when building new parts of the park. I don't understand much of what he says, but it makes him happy. By the time we're ready to move, Anaya has round up over thirty girls to follow her around the park decked out in their Disney best.

"Isn't it interesting how it actually looks like a wooden coaster if you stand back far enough?" Devin asks once we're sitting tight in a thirty minute queue line.

"It does, right?" I ask in amazement. "But it's not."

"No, it's not." Devin chuckles. Bethany and Bryan have befriended another couple who came out to hang with Anaya and so we've been abandoned.

"I really hope you land that internship, you know," I say, meaning it. "It'll be good for you. You'll be so happy." I squint against the sun, wishing there was a readily available indoor line.

"Thanks," Devin puts an arm around me. "Won't you miss me, though?"

I mull over the question. "I will, but I'll survive. It's not like you'll be gone. I'll just have to work with James more often than I'd like."

He sticks his tongue out. "Sorry."

"She's pretty fake," someone behind us whispers. Our eyes meet instinctually. "Like, okay, you really live and breathe Disney? You can't be that happy all the time. Definite act." Another voice chimes in and I move a hand to my mouth to mask the fact it has dropped open.

"Wow, Abigail, check that out," Devin takes my shoulders and turns me, pointing at a hidden Mickey perched on the coaster... which just happens to be in the direction of the two culprits. A few parties behind us are two girls who've come along for Anaya's meet up, bounding as Disney dogs, Perdita and Lady.

"Wow, cool," I say, obviously looking at them and not whatever else Devin had in store for me to see. I turn on my heel and give him a look that tells him I am ready to throw down.

"Relax, don't say anything just yet." He shakes his head at me, eyes willing me to tone it down a notch.

"That one's her friend, I think. She's probably just as bad." They go on. Now my mouth really drops open.

"Okay, she is *not* as bad." Devin bellows. Their voices go to tittering whispers and then halt. My eyes shoot open wide.

"Dev," I chide, biting back a smile.

"What? It's true. You want to say something? Try whispering." He guffaws and I actually let out a laugh. They are silent behind us, or at least quiet enough for us not to hear.

"You are the worst." I tremble with laughter.

"You love it."

"Yeah, yeah,"

After our ride, we plan to inform Anaya that she has a few haters, but lucky for us, the girls solve the problem themselves by leaving quietly. In their place, though, come fellow Disney influencers.

"If you thought that was bad, it's about to get way worse," I grumble at Devin as Ashley, Instagram's favorite Disney makeup artist, enters our view in full-on Bo Peep garb. She's done her eyes up a soft pink that transcends into a shimmering blue with compliments by her artificial lashes and a shepherdess crook drawn elegantly across her face. She has overdone it, but that is exactly what this community lives for. If she's going for discreet, that plan flies out the window when she practically screeches with joy upon making eye contact with Anaya, who is looking back at her like she's never had a better Dis-friend in the world.

"You really can't hide your facial expressions, can you?" Devin whispers close to me over the bite into his macaroni and cheese cone.

"I'm not sure that I try all that hard," I joke. Ashley and Anaya are catching up, discussing algorithms and past Instagram stars who are no more. Meanwhile, the group of non-online-famous women watch in awe. All for the exception of Bethany, who has a look that mirrors mine as she directs her prudence at me.

"I know," I mouth, nodding my head. She rolls her eyes in response, clasping her hands together and twirling in a make-shift impersonation of Ashley and her holier than though act.

I snort, walking around the group of mindless zombies and taking in the surroundings of Cars Land. *Pandora or Cars Land? Hmm. Still undecided.*

"We should at least get a picture while we're waiting for Anaya to wax the floor Ashley walks on," Bethany whips out a digital camera, truly an ancient relic, and points it at Mater and Lightning McQueen just behind us. They'd pulled up a few moments earlier, revving their engines in greeting, but our party of thirty-something was too busy enjoying the good life to notice.

"That'll be a cute one," I nod, taking Devin by the hand and propping us on Mater's hood. Bethany locates a park guest to snap our shot and jogs to Lightning, Bryan trailing closely behind, connecting us all with her and my joined hands.

Like clockwork, we've gathered the attention of at least half the group as Anaya's closest friends, and all at once, the others also want their photo with the two stars of *Cars*.

We go from being models to professional photographers in seconds, all of us dumbfounded as we're asked to turn cameras this way and that. It's difficult to restrain the laughter building in my throat, because all these girls must think we're masters of the craft, when really we have no absolute idea what it is that is being asked of us. If only we had Aaron to help us now.

Girls are slouching on the cars, putting their hands to their brows, holding strands of their hair up like accessories. It is absolute chaos and is pretty damn hilarious.

"You know, I'm all about the feminist agenda," Devin starts once we've finished embarrassing ourselves on hands and knees for the perfect image. I pin him with a glare so he can keep whatever offensive comment that's coming next to himself. "And you ladies are killing it?" He puts his hands up, points at me questioningly.

"Good one," Bethany shrugs, Bryan quiet as can be beside her.

"How are you enjoying yourself, Bryan?" I ask, feeling nicer than usual and sorry for the whole lot of us.

"I honestly love it here, this place personally doesn't hold a candle to Disney World, but I'm digging the vibes." He smiles kindly at me, making me feel like a jerk all the more.

"Right, the vibes," I raise my brows.

"We were thinking of going to the Santa Monica pier tonight, actually," Bethany takes his arm. I mentally question the state of their relationship and whether he's admitted that he's, you know, made out with her roommate and also best friend. Just curious.

"Maybe we'll join you," Devin prompts and I purse my lips.

"Or maybe we can do something else," I say pointedly, so that he can get the hint that while I don't fancy Bryan at all, I'd like to let Bethany have some time with him on her own. "Anyways," I say, before anyone can raise any other questions. "Are we hopping over to Magic Kingdom or what?"

"I'm trying to be nice," I hold a hand to my forehead, mentally willing the sounds of Anaya and Ashley's cackling out of my head. I'm not jealous, I don't think, but some people just don't rub well on me. Top that off with the fact that Anaya has just recently posted my spontaneous teacup picture and now my phone is getting Instagram notifications off the chart? Yeah, not great.

In the midst of this unsolicited chaos, the sounds of Dapper Dans write the soundtrack to my soul. I've come to decide Magic Kingdom is still my preferred park of choice even here in California. There's just something about Main Street U.S.A.

"Try harder," Bethany wills me to pull it together, but Devin is also silently chuckling behind her and I can't keep a serious face when he's holding a hand so tight on his mouth it looks like he can't breathe. I watch him, eyes wide, and he looks like he's going to burst when he removes his hand.

"*Sephora just liked my photo, I think I have reached* peak." Devin flaps his hands around in what's supposed to be a prissy impersonation and we all just about lose it.

"We are bad friends!" Bethany heaves, hands on knees as *AnayasBigDayatDCA* group hurriedly marches on without us. If she had asked, I would have told Anaya I think the hashtag is a little too long to be able to follow, but she didn't, so now we must both suffer.

"True," I wipe at my eyes, prickling with tears from the laughter.

"You're one to talk, Abby, you're all over the Disney internet right now." Bryan directs his humor at me, eyes dancing between Devin and me. I flash him a scowl. He can roll with the punches when he isn't being quiet, I take it.

"Stay out of this," I point, still laughing.

"Do you guys mind passing out the goodies now?" Ashley comes over, presenting us with a basket of sparkling gifts and interrupting the most fun we've had all day. I feel myself border on the edge of snarky, to only then ask myself what I might do if I were on the clock right now.

"Sure thing," Devin interjects, snatching the basket before I can think of something smart to say. "We'll do that right now." Her smile is snakelike, untrustworthy by nature and I feel my skin crawl at the sight of her overly done rose blush. While I'm certain that Ashley's sole purpose in life is to sabotage Anaya while posing as one of her closest Instagram friends, I'd never say as such out loud. I try to conjure up a smile for her but it feels harsh and unnatural on my face. The way she flicks her hair over her shoulder and turns on her heel tells me the feeling is mutual.

"What, she can't hand them out herself?" I say once she's far enough to not hear. The way she stumbles in her heels tells me that she doesn't walk in them enough to know how to do it properly.

"We came here to help, you know that." Bethany laughs, fisting a few of the gift bags and throwing them into her own purse. When she catches my accusing glare, she shrugs. "Can't pass up the chance at some free stuff."

"Did Anaya do some of these?" Devin wafts through the picnic basket, surprised at some of the items he comes across. "There are some pretty cool key chains in here."

"No, she didn't. I knew she was trying to sabotage her." I say matter-of-factly and everyone emits a synonymous sigh of disagreement. "Anyways, tell everyone the gifts are from the both of them." I grab a fistful of bags and go on my merry way before they can launch into a heated discussion as to why I am wrong.

As I make my way through the crowd, girls left and right do their best to look at me without looking my way, eager to get their hands on whatever the Instagram gods have decided to grace them with. "From Anaya," I say cheerily to some. "From Anaya and Ashley." To others. This is as close as I come to being diabolical.

"Your Grumpy is showing," Devin comes close behind me, handing over his last of party favors to a group of girls who are inspecting the wrapping like it may still have traces of gold left in the packaging.

"How kind of you," I lift a shoulder, grinning ear-to-ear the way I do every day for park guests.

"That's low, Abby. Your Disney smile? Come on." Devin clucks his tongue.

"It comes naturally," I laugh, waving at the girls as we stride off to the back of the crowd so that they can continue with their Main Street photoshoot.

Devin sets the basket on the ground and puts both hands on my shoulders. "How do you feel about the prospect of disappearing?"

I eye him quizzically, crossing my arms at the waist. "Please explain the nature of said prospect."

"Right, well," he glances both ways in full-on spy mode. I hold back a laugh. "Right behind us is the Main Street Cinema. In just a few steps, we can easily become untraceable."

"How will we ever cover our trail, Bond?" I roll my eyes, secretly giddy at the thought of taking off, never to be seen at this Big Day again.

"Uncertain, but we've got to take a chance. What say you?" Devin pulls me to him tightly in an attempt to shield me from the eyes of possible onlookers.

"I'm outta here," I say, untangling myself from his hold and darting for the production of Steamboat Willie.

"I am thoroughly enjoying this AC but figured there would be actual seating," I mumble, but Devin is too entranced by the vintage production to compute my words.

"Take what you can get," he says, his mouth barely moving. Devin's appreciation of the company and all that has gone into it in all its years is admirable. I love Disney, but Devin loves the gears of Disney, every bit and piece that comes together to make every movie, every ride, every location. I fell in love with the magic that is put in front of each guest and the way I get to create it for them, but Devin...Devin is something more than that. He loves the *bones* of Disney.

He has always been the man fascinated with what's really going on behind scenes, how the magic came to be, how it'll continue to thrive. And beyond that all, he's found interest in me, the girl who does what she's told without asking questions. I'm trying to change that, though, maybe some for him, but mostly for me. I'm starting to find there's more than just being the good girl, more than just conformity.

"You're a great friend," I tell him as authentically as I know how. The room is dark around us, cool and empty as everyone else shuffles in and out of the theater as quick as they enter upon finding it's nothing but a few old television screens.

He is frozen, eyes glued to the screen until the credits roll, and then he turns to look at me, hands in his pockets, rocking on his heels. "You going to ask me what you really want to?"

Now it is my turn to be quiet. There are words on my lips, but too many to ask, and none of them border on important enough to voice. "Maybe."

"Oh," he tries his hardest not to look disappointed.

"Patience," I echo and we both laugh, the cinema quiet between us aside from the relaying sounds of Steamboat Willie, a violent contrast to the folly inside my mind.

* * *

How does one explain that they are too old for coy games of romance but also ignorant enough to tolerate them longer than they should? All in all, that is the embodiment of my current state of mind and I really should get around to saying something. And I might, I just might, if "Kiss the Girl" was not playing all around us. In fact, I've planned a few viable options.

So, are you going to do it?

I'm waiting.

Any day now.

"Care to explain the technological specialties of this ride?" I utter instead, willing myself not to slap my own face as he leaps into uncensored discussion.

"So this ride is kind of the first of its own due to the use of...." He starts, hands clenching and pointing between Eric and Ariel, who happen to be acting out exactly what we could be doing right now. Oh, irony, how you mock me so.

He goes on to discuss the level of intricacy that goes into the new technology of animatronics, the expense of specific equipment and the amount of electricity that is powered into the ride, combated by solar panels.

I am in awe at the depth of his knowledge, entranced by something I don't quite completely understand. How have I failed to see that Devin is brilliant? And, why, thinking back, did conversation always drift more towards my interests? Have I been neglecting him of the typical rite of passage that comes with friendships? Do I suck?

"Do I suck?" Also comes out of my mouth, but by this point in time I'm not all too surprised that I've lost control of most verbal output in front of Devin. I'm sure he could somehow explain this to me, too.

"What?" He stops mid-discussion, hands slowly sinking to his lap.

"We've been friends all this time and yet I feel like I rarely see you get this detailed about what you love."

"You're crazy," Devin chuckles, tugging my hands now sadly splayed in front of me. "You know everything about me, you just don't allow me to fully express my nerdom the way you should," he's only joking but it doesn't help my emotional mindset much.

I think, mentally willing information to pop into my brain, and Devin is right, I do know most about him: his likes, his dislikes; favorite food (lasagna), favorite video game (Kingdom Hearts, but we work at Disney, are you surprised?), the works.

"Remind me to let you quiz me later," I chide lightly and he lets it drop.

"It's a date," he pops out of our clamshell and bows, holding his hand out for me to take. I blush at the sight of others watching our interaction as we exit the ride, but when I take his hand, I don't let it go.

"I think," I say, holding in a breath. Devin is still walking, coolly enjoying the presence of my hand in his. "I've been very, very, neglectful of your feelings."

This...this stops him. Quickly, too.

"I wouldn't say that," he assures me, propping me up against a wall so that others can continue down the nautical platform onto their next ride.

"For a while I thought that maybe all these feelings were new, but part of me is starting to think I've always had them and I've been, I don't know, oblivious. You've just been my friend for so long. Why did you never tell me?" I bite my lip, eyes on his collarbone because I'm too afraid to see his reaction.

"For that very reason," he tilts my chin up. "You're my friend first, Abigail. I figured when you wanted to notice that I'm crazy about you, you would." Our eyes lock, his full of longing, and mine, well, I'm not quite sure, but it can't be that dissimilar.

"So, you are?" I grin wildly. "Crazy about me?"

"Redundant question." He tilts his head towards mine and my heart is galloping in my rib cage. "What I'm really wondering is how exactly you feel about me?"

"If you're still wondering—" I start, using my free hand to pull him closer, just as the start of the *Avengers* theme begins to play from his pocket. Devin rests his forehead against mine with a sigh and brings his phone to his ear. We've been caught.

"We're a bit busy, but, aha, yep, alright, you've got it, we'll be there." He rolls his eyes, clicking off the phone and pocketing the device. "Guess who,"

"Don't want to," I lean up and kiss his cheek. "We'll finish this later."

"Yeah?" he looks down at me hopefully.

"Yeah."

"Bethany went out with Bryan," I notify Anaya, who looks like any possible slip-up tonight will be the absolute downfall of her relationship with the Disney community.

"Seriously?" she seethes, though I can't understand why it might matter that she only has the company of one friend.

"Yep, but I don't think I'm that bad, honestly." I shrug, assuming that this means it'll just be Anaya and I bonding over Disney trivia tonight at the Disneyland Hotel.

A few weeks ago, Anaya had been contacted to attend an exclusive event to try new food and beverage pairings that would soon be served at the California parks. We'd been to events of the likes in Orlando before and always left happily full, but I usually had Bethany to accompany me and I think it goes without saying that Anaya's friends and I are not the kind to get along so easily.

Anaya glares at me from her spot on the adjacent loveseat, a look I am all too familiar with. Phil Collins croons in the background to another mopey *Tarzan* song. I do my best to tune it out; the soundtrack always makes me cry. I meet her eyes with my own, equally as daunting, and before either of us can make a brutal dig at the other, a bedroom door opens and closes.

Devin saunters in, fresh out of the shower and looking like he's done with parks for the next few months. I know the feeling. I've had enough walking to last me several lifetimes. I don't think my feet have known a time where they weren't in pain in the past three years.

"I didn't know we were subjecting ourselves to Disney film torture tonight," Devin plops down next to me. "We're looking to cry, I see." He pouts at preteen Tarzan on the flat screen television.

"Nothing a good cry can't fix," Anaya drones, but she's already looking down at her cell, typing away and most likely making plans to match her next outfit to that of her other shallow Disney pals. I really am the jealous type, aren't I?

Maybe I'm also a little harsh, too. Anaya works her ass off so that she can look good online and keep her real-life persona together. She is the utmost definition of a boss babe, and I commend her for it. There isn't a thing she hasn't done to include Bethany and I in her quest for Disney domination. Maybe I shouldn't have run off today, but I don't necessarily regret it.

"Hey," Devin's voice knocks me out of my thoughts. "How about I take you out tonight?" He asks. My stomach bursts in a bout of knotted butterflies and my neck tingles with heat. He's looking at me like he's been thinking about asking for hours, and the sweet twinkle in his eye makes me want to kiss him on sight.

My eyes flit between him and Anaya, who is still entranced by whatever scandal is currently holding the online Disney community hostage. I could leave her to do her own bidding or I could quietly oblige and pay her back the only way I know how for the complimentary room, room service, and Disney treats we've been pampered with. You know, just be a decent friend, really. Devin won't go anywhere, will he?

"I would love to," I say regretfully, my hand tender on his arm. "But Anaya has this press event tonight, and I swore I'd go."

He mulls this over a moment, looking more forward-thinking than actually disappointed. "Okay," he says at least. "No rush." He reaches up to move a stray hair from my face. "How does tomorrow sound?"

His hand is still resting loosely along the edge of my face as I nod eagerly.

"I feel like a princess," I gasp in surprise at what Anaya has selected for me to wear for the event coverage.

"A princess gone rogue, more like it." Anaya's head tilts at the mirror, watching me twist and turn in the glitzy wine number. Every which way I try, another layered shade of plum encompasses me in a dazzling, gala style gown.

"But is this too much?" I breathe, mentally willing it not to be. This is the most lovely dress Anaya has ever graced me with borrowing.

"Who cares? I love being too much. It's a mood." Her excitement is palpable, and in her own mesmerizing green garb, we look like match made foes.

The press event is made of dreams, with photo booths at check-in, complimentary goodie bags with covetable Disney merch, and of course, endless food. Color me impressed. It's crazy to think that within such a short span of time, Disney has gone from being a company shrouded in mystery to one that allows online personalities to help decide and voice opinions at the park. It still doesn't make complete sense to me, but if exploiting myself online for the sake of it is what must be done, looks like I'm a total sellout.

The convention center has been decked out to give the appearance of a villainous hangout, with according devious lighting, character meet and greets, and a Hades-esque DJ who isn't doing a shabby job. Anaya's choice for our attire makes much more sense now, as I am donning the purple hues of Maleficent while she models the complementing green. We are quite the pair to be messed with, and everyone is absolutely enjoying telling us so as we make our way across the room.

"This is a great outfit," I tell her when she stops another individual of the press to take our photo. We switch up a few poses before he's done a job acceptable enough for Anaya, and then we are going back and forth to get our own close-ups. In between, Anaya is tapping away at her device; I very thinly stop myself from whacking it out of her hand.

"How do you feel about being overdressed now? Isn't it awesome?" She says, looking up from her phone and nodding at me.

"It is, especially since I don't ever dress this nice." I shrug, pulling out my own phone from my clutch. "Take a Boomerang of me...I feel like this needs to be documented."

"Are you asking me to do something to help better your media handles? Wow. I am pleasantly surprised." Anaya jumps on her heels, fingers eager to be the one behind the lens as she so rarely is. "Twirl for me, girl."

"Done," I say, grinning as I do.

"I didn't thank you for helping earlier today," Anaya says when we've finally taken our seats at the table that, luckily, does not include most of Anaya's internet passé. "I really appreciate it, you guys always being around to deal with the madness." Her hand is on my arm as I take it and squeeze.

"It really isn't a problem," I tell her. "Sorry that I kind of disappeared today."

"About that," she snaps a photo of the rose gold wine we've been given to sample, something new coming for the spring season. "Tell me everything."

"Nothing to tell," I purse my lips but go on to explain every excruciating detail like a schoolgirl, regardless.

"We're a bit old to be playing at this, aren't we, Abigail?" Anaya laughs good naturedly, bringing the drink to her lips. "Just mack him already."

"Every time I try, you somehow interrupt!" I shove her.

"Not true!" She howls.

"True! We have bad timing, is all." I whisper, wondering if it's a sign that maybe it's too good to be true.

"Did you just play that card on me? You have got to be joking!" Anaya sets down her rose gold drink as if it's poison, winning us a few looks from other Disney bloggers who do not look all too enthusiastic about her participation at the event. Why must everyone be so catty?

"I might have," I try my best to keep the remorse out of my tone.

"Devin has been after you since before you'd even really looked in his direction. Don't you remember all the times he came over asking to take you to the parks? And when he'd drive us to the mall when no one had a car? Or, oh, I don't know, how he is always paying for your food?" Anaya ends with an argument I can't exactly get behind but I nod along anyways because she looks absolutely appalled and I refuse to get her even more riled up.

"Devin is just a good guy, and a great friend. That's all been out of kindness." I assure her, though I'm working to do more for myself. Once again, I'm left questioning the validity of my sight...and reason.

"I'm willing to bet there was more to it than just being a nice guy, which he is." She says, for once without a hand on her phone or any other inanimate object nearby. The sternness of her words add on to the uncertainty in my stomach, and we let the conversation drop, because if we're going to have this one, then we also need to discuss Bethany.

"You've been on your phone all night. Is there some serious drama I should know about?" I reach for the wine, marveling at the fact that it contains edible glitter (which is questionable) and take a small sip.

"Actually, no. I've been working on something." Her voice rises with excitement, and when she reaches for her phone, it isn't Instagram I'm looking at, but a website. It's bubbling with color and immaculate calligraphy, adorned with photos of us all together at the parks.

"You did this?" I scramble for her phone, in awe of what she's done.

"I'm working on it, here's the first blog post I'm writing." She clicks a few times and then I'm on a page telling me about everything I can do at Walt Disney World on a budget.

"This is amazing," I laugh. "I'm so proud of you." I shake my head. I never thought Anaya would actually take our ideas to heart, but here she is, putting her best foot forward. I should have known better.

"It's not done," she swats my hand. "But it's coming along. I was actually wondering if you might like to edit it once I'm finished."

"What? Yes, of course." There is a buzz of pure bliss in my head. I'm so happy for her, and being able to help make this come to life? Cherry on top. I can't help but draw her in for a hug.

"You girls are so sweet," someone next to us chimes in and we pull apart, eyeing each other questionably. "I'm Deena, I follow you on Instagram. I really admire your content."

We twist in our seats and are greeted by a much older woman with round spectacles and an impressive amount of food in front of her. She smiles warmly at us, her face openly curious.

"Thanks," we say in unison, though I'm not sure she's talking to me.

"I really loved the photo the company posted of you today." Now, her eyes are on me.

"Huh?" My words slip before I think to formulate a reputable sentence, winning me an interrogatory look from this woman.

"Wait...*what*?" Anaya is next to voice her shock, but she is quicker than lightning, instantaneously clicking away at her phone. "Holy...oh, man."

All at once, Deena seems to put together that we are both bumbling idiots, emitting a small laugh that I can't seem to follow for the life of me.

"Abigail, do not outright lose your mind. Okay? Okay." Anaya sounds like she's trying to talk herself down much more than she might be trying to talk me down.

She meets my eyes inquiringly, but doesn't hand the phone over until I nod impatiently. "Just give it –Oh, *oh*, is that *me*?"

My face, smirking and cryptic, plastered on the official Disneyland Instagram page in my Mary Poppins dress, spinning madly in a teacup.

"Definitely, yes, you." Anaya is just as dumbfounded as our hands jointly cradle the screen before us. The photo shows as being shared over three hours ago.

"How did we not see this until now?" I breathe, a tinged mix of fear and excitement at my online exposure.

"Because," Anaya clicks on the photo once, already having liked it. A text bubble appears and shows that it is my account that has been tagged in the image. "They tagged *you*."

"Wow," I say, reaching for my phone at the same time as a multitude of followers flood my notifications. I'd already had enough on account of being Anaya's best friend, but now? I'll certainly have to monitor the sort of stuff I post. "Wow." I say, apparently at a loss of coherence.

Deena is nodding and laughing at us. "Shocked?"

"Barely," I roll my eyes in joke and she titters with laughter.

"It just got better," Anaya leans back into me, shoving my phone out of view and hers back in. She scrolls through the comments and lands on a familiar screen name followed by heart emoticons. "Devin commented."

"I would say 'wow' again, but at this point in conversation I think I should change it up." I shake my head in disbelief, fond of the attention but still too wound up at the thought of being publicized.

"I don't know who is more smitten – him or you! Just look at that. He's, like, publicly displaying his love for you online." Anaya's world has appeared to tilt on its access, and she looks just milliseconds from dropping money on the status of our maybe-lationship.

"Cat's out of the bag?" I propose with a half-shrug, already sorting through the tremendous amount of people who have suddenly decided to take interest in my life all because Disney has told them to. I can't say that I blame them after what a good job Aaron did of getting the money shot.

"Understatement," Anaya clucks, watching as I go through my new followers. "Let me see the Boomerang you posted."

I show her and she looks pleased with herself. "I'm getting a ton of messages over it."

"Ohhh, let's see." She takes my phone from my hand. "I'll weed out and block all the trolls."

"Be my guest," I sigh, knowing that with any sort of attention comes people who love to discredit you.

While Anaya does her dirty work, I learn that Deena works for one of the top Disney blogs online, one I can even say I myself follow. We go on to discuss our favorite Disney spots, which is always such an easy topic of conversation, and Deena says that Disneyland Paris is a hidden gem I must make a point of visiting. Our lighthearted conversation is quickly interrupted by another revelation, though.

"I'm just going to let you handle this." Anaya tosses me my cellular device with a knowing smirk. I'm about to tell her we can live off our phones for the next few hours when I see it.

Stunning.

One worded followed by a period from a guy I can't stop thinking about in response to me twirling in a larger-than-life dress.

"I'm going to be risqué." I say to myself.

Be careful, I might let that comment go to my head.

The moment the message sends, it shows as having been read by Devin. My heart is in my throat as a typing bubble appears and disappears over the next thirty seconds, and then, at last, two words appear.

Please do.

I am grinning like a madwoman the next few hours at the event, goofy in all social interactions and overly amused, all until we make our way back to the hotel suite.

I make sure to pinch my cheeks and check my makeup before entering the room again, expecting to catch a quick, if any, small sighting of Devin before being ushered to bed. When we do enter and I'm not so lucky, it's hard to mask my disappointment. Anaya wordlessly moves to hit the sack, but I stay behind, contemplating if I should attempt texting him just to see if luck may be on my side tonight? No. He did say we'd spend the day together tomorrow.

Just as I'm convinced I have no choice but to get to bed and hope for the best for the following day, I notice that the door to the balcony is propped open.

Tiptoeing, I'm quick to reach for the sliding glass door, but just before I can shut it close, a shining of string lights catch my eyes, followed by the sound of lulled music.

I step out, soundlessly shutting the door behind me. Lights have been strung across the small patio and music from a portable stereo is lofting through the balcony, and in the middle of it all is Devin in a red button-down and jeans.

"You," I say, crossing my arms and striding towards him.

"I thought you might be a little more excited to see me," Devin catches me in an embrace and guides me to the small two-seater candle lit table that's been set-up to the far right.

"I'm not great at verbally expressing myself, but I'm actually very excited to see you," I let him know as he sits across me, motioning to the array of snacks set before us.

"I wasn't sure this was going to work out without knowing how late you'd be out, but I would have kicked myself if I hadn't been able to see you in that dress tonight." He speaks with his head hanging low so that I can't see his eyes, and I know that even though his words come easily, he is embarrassed at voicing his thoughts so openly.

"Funny, I was just thinking something very similar about you seeing me in this." I tell him, reaching for a bagged chocolate chip cookie.

"Oh," he scratches the back of his neck, smiling brightly at me. The hiccup in my chest at his reaction surprises me more than it should. "I gathered the finest snacks provided by room service," he adds with a quick laugh.

"You're quite the charmer, Devin. Not sure if I've told you that." I bite into my treat, barely tasting the chocolate between my nerves.

"I don't exactly mind hearing it a few times over." He shrugs nonchalantly, so himself in the moment that it makes me wonder what I'm waiting for.

It is quiet between us, with only the sounds of the parks below us and the music around us. He's gone with a classical selection of Disney music, and as "Tale as Old as Time" closes, the main theme of *Up* begins.

"I love this song!" I say, jumping up. Devin follows suit, taking my hand.

"You asking me to dance?" he asks, but has already dropped his other hand around my waist and is moving us in small circles.

"I am," I whisper, leaning my head against his chest and feeling very suddenly safe and at ease. How in the world can one person do that? And, how, beyond it all, is that person quite possibly Devin for me?

"Did you have fun tonight?" he asks, his stubble rubbing against my forehead as he speaks.

"I did," I nod, going on to tell him about how Anaya and I discovered that an image of me had been posted on the Disney page.

"It's a great photo," Devin pulls me closer into what feels like a congratulatory hug and I lift my arms to his neck.

"I really like the comment you left, too," I lift a hand to his cheek just as he dips me.

"Heart eyes...It was a work of art, wasn't it?" Devin quips, laughing into my temple. I rear back with a guffaw.

"Sure," we both laugh. I can't imagine a time when I've been happier, and the feeling of content that is bubbling inside me now is one I want to stay for a long time to come.

"Don't act like it didn't send your heart over the moon." Devin twirls me, his voice softer, more somber as our dancing begins to slow.

"Over the moon? Maybe. The other comment you made sent me over the sun, though." I shrug, my attempt at flirting probably the lamest it can get.

"Way to nerd-flirt," He pulls me back into him, our noses brushing from the nearness.

I think of plenty of other intelligent things I can say about knowing much more about the solar system than I do about engineering, and how he has me feeling like I have the surface of both the moon and the sun locked up inside me right now, but it's all too elementary for me, and I can only think to ask what I really want to know.

"How long, Dev?" I bring his chin down to mine, our lips inches away from each other, feeling as though they're linked by an invisible thread between us.

His eyes are sober but hopeful as they search mine. I can't peg the point in time when I decided that Devin was a better companion than all the other contenders that had proceeded him, but I know now that the feeling I have for him means something entirely unique. There is elongated silence between us as he decides what to say.

"Always," he shakes his head against mine, releasing a deep sigh in uneasy anticipation.

And then, on my tiptoes, I kiss him, willing away all the uncertainties he may have felt just seconds before. It is soft and tentative at first, sweet and slow in execution, and then it becomes something more as fireworks are alight behind us. Some time passes before we break off, but when we do, we are giddy with smiles and laughs that can last for days.

"You want to hear something strange? I feel like I've been waiting forever for this." I admit, leaning against his chest, feeling the strong beat of his heart in his ribs.

"I know just what you mean," he ensures me, and we continue dancing and kissing until the fireworks are long gone and the music has ended. When we finally do part, my dreams are the sweetest I've ever had.

Eleven

Be back around noon. Anything in specific you wanted to do today?
Hmmm...something with you?

I'm floating on cloud nine, ying in bed well past a reasonable hour when I see the message from Devin. I'm not sure where he went, but I'm not too disappointed knowing it won't be long before he returns. There's also a missed call from Bethany from a few minutes ago, but I don't think much of it. The girls are probably just wondering what we'll be doing today, and they'll be plenty excited to hear I have something already planned.

Seeing that it's only ten till noon, I hastily throw on a casual top and jeans, shuffling around the suite until I come to terms with the fact that everyone has taken off for the day. Disappointed, I pick up my cell and open up our girls exclusive group chat.

Guess who's currently getting ready for a hot date with an old friend...

Minutes later, there's still no response from the girls, but Devin is walking in, brown paper bag in hand.

"Hey," I turn towards him, wringing my hands together in silent panic. How does one greet the guy she very recently admitted her true feelings to?

"Hey, yourself," Devin crosses the room in large strides, offering me the bag. "I wasn't sure you'd be out of bed yet, so I brought you a few things."

"Thanks," I peek inside, discovering an assortment of blueberry muffins and chocolate glazed donuts. All my favorites.

"I just ask that you share." His eyes flicker mischievously as he envelopes me in an embrace. My insides flip repetitively when I put the bag on the kitchen counter and hold tight to him.

"I will consider it," I tease, and before I can wonder what happens next, Devin's lips are on mine and I'm transported back to last night. It's just as exhilarating, thrilling as the first time. When we finally pull apart, we're both laughing shyly. "Okay, okay, I'll share."

"I have awesome news," Devin's hand in mine is firm and meaningful, somehow completely new from the way we've loosely held hands in the past. It's almost embarrassing to admit how much I'm enjoying this. I hope he doesn't ask about it. "I had a friend pull a few strings and long story short, we're going to do something extremely cool in a bit."

Today, the sky is overcast and I'm once again struck by the underwhelming size of the castle here at Disneyland as we stroll down Main Street U.S.A.. If Walt were still around, I might ask questions.

"Are we?" I quip, feinting a lack of enthusiasm if only to keep up my reputation as a stone cold woman.

In response, Devin only glares, mockingly upset. I'm about to rival his stare with an eyebrow raise when he abruptly lifts my hand above my head and spins me on my heel.

"Oh, yes," he says, pulling me back in close. I smile into his chest without question. Nothing wrong with feeling like a princess at Disneyland.

After an hour or so of bumbling around the park with no specific intentions other than to exchange shy smiles and enjoy the presence of each other, we rear back towards the front of the park and wait just outside of the Main Street fire station.

"What are we waiting for?" I ask as Devin furiously types on his cell phone.

"We're waiting for a who," Devin pockets it, scratching at his chin nervously.

"Hey, it's okay," I assure him, squeezing his hand. His shoulders noticeably lose their tension, but I've known Devin too long to assume he isn't a bit riled up. "What's going on?"

"I called in a favor to a friend."

"Yeah?" I wonder, watching the sky above us noticeably darken. If the weather here is anything like Florida, it'll be raining in the next few minutes, and frighteningly so.

"Well, a friend of a friend. Bethany's friend. That Jenna girl?" Devin looks at my face, but not really at me, and there is a small pang in my chest at the thought of whatever he had planned not going right.

"I'm sure everything's fine." I try to console him even more, knowing most of my words are useless, but as fate would have it, we are lucky today, and a few minutes later an older cast member wearing a cherry red dress and stilettos approaches us. By the looks of it, she might be a manager, decked out with her handy trash picker pin. Her nametag reads "Christine" and as she approaches, she does not break eye contact behind her darkly shaded lenses.

"Devin? Abigail?" She looks between us professionally, not breaking show or giving me a reason to question her level of importance to the company. In just two words, I can tell she's been here awhile. The outstretched Mickey on her nametag reaffirms my guesses: she's been with the company for at least twenty years.

"Christy? Hi!" Devin takes a hand out for her to shake and I follow suit.

"So nice to meet you two, have you been enjoying the park?" She speaks with us nonchalantly, quietly leading the way to something I still haven't quite pegged. Devin is quick to launch into discussion about the differences between Disneyland and Disney World, admiring both of their individual assets and detailing how much he's enjoyed seeing the Galaxy's Edge expansion. Holy hell, is he a big time nerd.

Christine takes us behind set discreetly, wiring us up a set of ladders that lead to a small hallway just above the fire department, and then into...

"Welcome to Walt's apartment."

A quaintly outdated room of priceless antiques stretches out before us in what must only be the very specific taste of the man who started it all.

"Devin," I breathe, sure that I must be swaying on my feet planted firmly before the opening. Christine does her best to not appear as amused as she most definitely is, but I am in utter and complete shock. "You...what?"

Devin, on the other hand, does nothing to hide the look of smugness that naturally emits from his childlike face upon my reaction. "You're welcome," he says simply, taking my elbow and gently steering me inside.

The girls will have an absolute field day when they hear about this.

Christine, though, does not miss a beat, and launches into animated discussion about the apartment. We learn that it is roughly 500 feet, due to the fact that it is nesting upon the fire station and inevitably did not have enough space to add on a room. It simply holds a restroom, kitchenette, family room, and a desk where Walt loved to work on off days. The apartment was decorated by the original designer of Main Street U.S.A. and set designer of multiple respectable live-action Disney films, Emile Kuri, and was cleverly built to match the interior of the firehouse; though most furniture has since been replaced, you still get that feeling.

Surprisingly, a small closet is situated in the apartment, and inside it is nothing other than a fire pole. While it was once open and welcome to use, it now lies sealed as to prevent any willing guests.

"It's a great thing they did that, if not Devin would be having a great time." I nudge his hip with my own, relishing in all the additional knowledge I'm picking up on thanks to his eager questioning. Where he asks, I like to simply listen in.

"These antiques are astounding. Is there any reason behind the choosing of them?"

"Simply pieces they enjoyed and found covetable while traveling."

"Did Mr. Disney have a favorite ride here?"

"It was often changing."

"Did Disney himself use that fire pole often?" This, of course, is where I interrupt.

"Told you the pole would be a problem for this one." I lift a finger, steering him in the opposite direction of the closet.

Christine titters with laughter, clearly enjoying Devin's enthusiasm and my playful shenanigans. "No, he liked more often than not to watch others use it, though I'm sure he liked to sparingly use it on his own."

"See, top bosses don't fool around with all the toys." I tease and we carefully enjoy the rest of our tour.

The thought of Devin doing something so utterly amazing for a girl who only told him the night before she truly has feelings for him is beyond me, but I am so, so appreciative, and of course, at a loss of how to repay the favor.

Before we're escorted out of the room, Christine snaps a few shots of us sitting in the parlor, and I know that I'll hold dearly to the only souvenir and memory I'll have of this place. It isn't every day that you get a personal tour of the premises.

"Devin, Devin, Devin," I croon, once we've said our goodbyes and are strolling out of the park hand in hand. "When were you planning on telling me that you are the ultimate date location spotter?"

"I never would self-proclaim that title, but now that you've given it to me, I think I'll roll with it." He pumps his arm in triumph and I roll my eyes. I have pampered his ego, and that, I think, is thanks enough.

Back at the hotel, we enjoy the emptiness of our suite and spend the next few hours huddled up on the couch, flicking between cooking (his favorite) and home improvement (my favorite) shows. Between short naps and stolen kisses, the afternoon is a picture perfect escape from the parks after the past few whacky days.

Hours pass with no reply from the girls, even when I post Devin's and my apartment photo on Instagram. Hundreds of other followers have decided the content is both like and comment worthy. Speculations as to whether Devin and I are an item run madly online, and users are tagging their friends telling them to look at what I've posted. Who would have thought that Anaya's goons were this much interested in my life as well? Can't say I despise the attention just yet.

In the midst of this, I turn to Devin and say, "Can you believe the girls haven't said anything?"

Devin, transfixed on the styling of Guy Fieri's overly compensating eating habits, pulls me closer to him. "What did you say to them?"

"Oh," I blanch. "I, nothing." I shrug, mentally willing myself to not be completely emotionally transparent, just once. Or, I could be honest. *Oh, you know, just told them that you are one hell of a kisser, and that you planned the best date I will probably ever have in the history of dates, and that you might, kind of, sort of, possibly be my boyfriend now?*

Again, how old am I?

"Don't buy that," he jokes, but he's kind enough to not press. He's a wise man, after all, respecting the secrets of women.

Curiously, I head to Anaya's Instagram page, hoping that'll give me the intel I need about what her whereabouts today are. Oddly enough, no new images have been posted and no new stories have been added.

Before I can convince myself that I am not a prime example of what it is to be paranoid, I voice my worries. "I think something's wrong."

Devin, again, is very easily distracted and simply shakes his head. "I spoke to Bethany earlier today about meeting up with Christine. She was curt, but, well, fine."

"She talked to you? But didn't answer my message?" I push aside the pang in my chest at being tossed aside like a candy wrapper and continue to snoop through Anaya's page, searching for the last time she was online: three hours ago, and the last comment she made on a post: last night.

Then, something I never thought I'd see stops me in my tracks.

"Fucking slut." I choke on my words, and this, thankfully, emits a choking cough from Devin.

"Jeez," he starts, but I'm shaking my head, blooding pumping through my sockets and clouding my vision.

"Dumb bitch." I say now, and Devin really gets a kick out of this, eyes bulging in concern. I keep reading through words too harsh to fully digest, especially since they're being directed at one of my few best friends.

Devin is quiet, peering over my shoulder in question but allowing me the time it takes to process that something vile has been done to target her. Shakily, I drag my thumb across the screen, clicking away to her tagged photos, and there, I find it.

Anaya, chest to chest with no one other than dimwit specialist, Bryan.

"Holy," Devin winces in lieu of the thousands of questions burning on his lips.

Picture after picture documents the same encounter, impossible to locate who was the one that started the leak.

Looks like Disney's cleanest influencer still likes to get down and dirty, huh?

What kind of friend does this to someone she claims to be like a "sister"?

Goes to show you, not all of the Disney community is sunshine and rainbows!

Surprised? Disfluencers are all. F A K E.

The comments and captions rage on as people argue as to whether Anaya is really so much holier than though, but what stumps me is how everyone has put together the fact that Bryan is linked to Beth...

"How do people put this shit together?" I seethe, eyes seeing red as I jump back and forth between tags and profiles, and then, finally, land on Bethany's page, where seldom few photos feature Bryan, though the ones that do certainly give the appearance that they might be together. When did I miss that?

Quickly, relief fills me as I realize I've yet to be dragged into the online drama, but just as fast, guilt overcomes me, as well.

"Can't keep anything from the internet now-a-days, Abby," Devin releases a sigh, knowing we've been at the brunt of the same damage before.

But this? I know this will be the scandal to withstand it all. This is absolute social sabotage, and whoever started it knows that. Who would hold onto a photo for months and then choose to post it only when we're suddenly being featured by both brands and Disney alike?

"Has Bethany seen this?" I'm nearly wailing as the front door suddenly swings open and shut.

I've summoned the devil incarnate. Her eyes are bloodshot, red-rimmed and tired. Her navy blouse is doused in water that I can only assume has come from the truth of a close friend's betrayal. She looks like she has nothing to lose.

"Yes, she has," She snorts deviously and is about to storm off to her room when she stops in her track. "And just so you know?"

"Oh man," I hear Devin whisper under his breath as she points her finger straight at me and jabs it in the air.

Everything that comes next seems to play in slow motion in my head.

"I know that you knew about that. How could you? My own best friend hide something like that from me. Do you know how embarrassed I am?"

"I...I don't," I stumble over my words, lips trembling as I deliver my response. What else can I say to her that won't peg me to be the villain? That I'm sorry I kept this secret for months? That I didn't beg Anaya to tell the truth (I did)? That I wasn't a better friend?

"Of course not," she shakes her head, promptly slamming the bedroom door behind her.

For minutes or what feels like hours, I stare at that door, hoping it will open, willing previous events to undo themselves, but I know none of the aforementioned is likely to happen.

Devin, for once, is quiet beside me with nothing to say. Did he know about what went on between Anaya and Bryan? Yes, but only because Bryan had fessed up and then I coaxed the truth out of him. While I'm sure that Bethany does not hold Devin accountable the way she does me, I can't help but feel that everyone on this trip has taken on a role of the guilty party.

"She's not going to come back out, Abigail." Devin says, maybe when I've gone on too long living in my own head and watching the bedroom door. "Just give her some space."

"Okay," I reply numbly, and then, beyond my comprehension, lift myself to my feet and drag myself to my own bedroom.

Sometime later, Devin follows me in with a plate at hand. On it is his world famous, normally irresistible, fried peanut butter and jelly sandwich. It looks delightful, but the thought of food, or anything else for that matter, reminds me of betrayal and the fact that I just can't stomach anything. Regardless, he lays with me and tells me that everything will be alright. For now, it's just enough.

As the sun goes down, I find that I can't take much of my self-hatred any longer. Gently, I present myself at Bethany's door, looking very much her alter-ego from earlier in my ratty pants and tear-stained shirt. I knock. And then I wait. And I wait. And I wait. It isn't enough.

I go back to Devin, lie under the covers and cry into his chest as he holds me tenderly, his silent pleas for me to calm down all that keeps me loosely glued together. Eventually, my eyes burn enough to convince myself that I am tired.

Before the world falls away, I mentally will the power of technology to work in my favor.

Bethany, words can't explain just how sorry I am. Please, let's talk.

Twelve

The way the sun hits just the right away when Devin turns his face toward mine makes the breath hitch in my throat. His raven black hair is sprawled across his pillow and forehead, arm slung behind his head. I want nothing more than to pull him closer and stay in bed all day, but the recollection of last night rids me of the thought.

I have helped sabotage the relationship between my best friends and I, and as of now, none of us are on speaking terms. I can't piece together when or how I fell asleep, but I vividly remember the drugging effect of Dev's sweet whispers and assurances. The fusion of hurt and gratefulness is gut-wrenching in my belly.

I move to swing an arm over his chest, but just as I do, the bedroom door comes crashing open, sending me to jump up in a gasp. I do my best to hide my disappointment that it isn't Bethany who has chosen to barge in, but Anaya herself does not look too well, either.

"It's our last day here," she saunters past the bed, barely registering that I am not alone in it or that Devin and I have finally quit playing our game of cat and mouse. I guess that was a discussion that would be on hold for a time. "Get up."

The thought of getting out of bed or doing anything other than wallowing in self-pity today is enough to emit a soft groan from my throat, but in an attempt to reinstate myself to Decent Friend, I lift myself to my feet.

"So she isn't speaking to you, either?" I ask, our Uber driver sneaking glances at us in the rearview mirror every few beats. "Did she at least hear you out?"

"Yes and no, the photo speaks for itself." Anaya shrugs, all too much like she's said her peace and is over attempting to defend herself.

When Devin let me know he'd be spending today with Bethany instead of joining us on our tacky tourist inspection of Los Angeles, I was a bit jealous, but then promptly recognized that there is no one else in our passé that Bethany is currently on speaking terms with. He has yet to reach out to me, and my skin crawls with each moment that passes where I don't know what Bethany is thinking or feeling.

"I just don't get why someone would purposely release a photo like that, or save it at all instead of just posting it when everything happened." I pick at the tip of my fingers, aggravated at the anxious tick.

Anaya is quiet, savoring the rugged streets of L.A. on our way to our first stop.

Minutes pass, and when she finally looks at me, her eyes are rimmed with tears. "The internet is not our friend."

The rest of the ride is silent, and when we finally land at the Walk of Fame, Anaya is sunglass clad and completely unreadable.

We quietly trek along the streets, glancing down at the pavement and occasionally snapping the shot of a long forgotten celebrity. We continue on like that, quietly embracing our own lurid thoughts until we reach the star chronicling Walt Disney himself.

"Here, let me get a photo of you with the plaque," Anaya whips out her phone for the first time today and I get down on one knee, but my heart isn't in it. "Awesome, this is a great one. I'm going to send it to Devin." It's the first time that she smiles with her teeth and I don't take it lightly.

"I'll get you, too." I encourage her to switch me off, but she doesn't remove her shades when I move to take the photo.

We stand quietly a little longer, contemplating the legacy that one man happened to leave all over the world...the man that brought us all together.

"You know, it's crazy. He was the definition of greatness, and yet he valued so much more than just being great. He loved his family, he genuinely loved his theme park...He did it all." Anaya's voice quivers and I can't help but feel that if some people peeked into our lives, they'd think we were a bit, well, insane. What's there to say, though? Once you work for the mouse, anything Walt Disney will get you pretty misty-eyed.

"It's amazing, is what it is. Isn't that why we all wanted to work for him in the first place?" I cross my arms over my chest. I expected our last day to be bittersweet, but this day is turning out to be much worse than bitter and not at all sweet.

Anaya huffs a breath before twisting on her heel and walking away. In the very obscure distance is the Chinese Theatre. I damn her with an eye roll.

"Bye, Walt," I whisper a wave before following. The walk to the theater is long and sweat inducing. I busy myself with thoughts on how to solve whatever it is that has unraveled us all, but there's no solution in sight. What Anaya and I did was wrong, plain and simple.

All we can do is hope that time can heal, but if she won't let me explain myself, it never will. I hurriedly push that thought away and instead try to enjoy the oddly off beaten look Hollywood has going for it. I figure its prime was maybe a century overdo, but it is still charmingly vintage, none the less.

Contrarily, the Chinese Theatre is rather impressive, and what is even more impressive is how Walt Disney Imagineering managed to orchestrate a spot-on representation back home at Hollywood Studios. I text Devin as such.

Quick Note: WDW Imagineering has outdone itself, truly.

A few seconds pass before word bubbles appear moments before his response. *You think?!?!*

I smile at the screen before pocketing the device and directing my attention to the theatre. It is full of magnificent shades of gothic red and iridescent gold, adorned with jet black inklings that top off a classic, clean look. If Devin were here, I'd sure he'd be able to give us insight on the history of its creation, but in his absence, we are silenced in wonder.

"I think that lately I have been too focused on trying to be great." Anaya simply says, stopping a few beats. "I haven't taken into consideration everything else that goes with that."

I consider her words before speaking. "In what sense?"

She snorts. "I think I've been so wrapped up in building a page and being a talked-about Disney entity that I haven't thought to consider if it was hurting my relationship with you guys. Plus, I've been selfish. I don't know what made me think keeping something like that from Bethany was a good idea."

"It was both of our faults. I could have said something at any time within the last three months. You can't just blame yourself." I wince at the thought. What would have been worse? My exposure then, or the gas lighting now?

"I wouldn't have let you say anything. You know that. It isn't your fault...I kept you quiet and I shouldn't have done that. I was a coward, and I told Beth as much, but she didn't want to hear it." Anaya looks like she is holding back so much more that she'd like to say, but instead, she waits quietly. I have nothing else to say because she's right.

"Sorry," is all that I can offer.

She shakes her head all the sudden, releasing herself of a trance and slugs an arm around my shoulder. "Anyways, you have some 'splaining to do! Devin and you? Tell me *everything*."

And so, I do.

After a trip to Hollywood Forever Cemetery, Santa Monica Pier, and the Griffith Observatory, Anaya and I decide that we've seen enough of California for one day and head back to the hotel. This particular evening, it is not empty, but Bethany does her best to avoid us and Bryan appears to be terrified to even sneak a glance at us.

"I'm very uncomfortable." I tell Devin when he wanders into my room and we can have some privacy.

"Everyone is," he gives me a pitiful smile and I swat his arm, though he catches it and uses it to his advantage to bring me closer.

"I think I'm about ready to go home. This trip's worn thin on me." I sigh, relaxing into his embrace.

"Don't say that," he chuckles. "We've still got fireworks to get to."

"Oh no," I groan.

At DCA, we wait patiently at the World of Color dessert party Bethany was lucky enough to snag for us last minute. Why she chose to include us in any of this, I don't understand, but something tells me it was with the help of Devin, who was the one to deliver the news to us. Aside from that, we'd been completely severed.

Bethany has latched onto Bryan for dear life and chosen him as the sole person to communicate with tonight. She does not dare make eye contact with any of us, and my anger must be palpable because beside me, Devin takes the hand I have clenched into a fist and smooths out my palm.

"I did something," Anaya clears her throat, winning over the attention of everyone at the table. We all wait silently as she lifts her chin shakily and states, "I deactivated by account."

"You...no," I scowl, sure that I may have simply just heard her incorrectly.

"What?" Bethany deadpans, but everyone is much too invested in Anaya's new revelation to really take notice that she has addressed us for the first time today.

"I was starting to get all the kind of attention I've been trying to avoid. I'm going to take some time off, and then maybe in a month or so, when all of this has settled, I'll start new."

"I think that's probably best," Devin chimes in. I don't disagree, but it's a lot to process. Anaya has worked on this for years, why give up so easily?

"I second that," Bryan adds, a bit riskily of him. Bethany's mouth is still parted open, but now she is shaking her head.

"I'm going to the bathroom," she excuses herself and I take it as my open, following her through the throng of people eager to get their hands on green macarons and chocolate truffles.

"Beth, wait, please," I reach for her arm but she shrugs me off. "Just give me a minute, that's all I ask." I beg, and when she turns to look at me, the hurt in her eyes is unmistakable. We have shattered her. Who would have thought she cared this much about Bryan?

"What, Abigail? What do you have to say that I don't know?" She lifts her arms in question, fueling my anger.

"Why is he any less guilty than me?" I throw the words at her before I can think better of them, but it is one of the most prevalent questions I have swimming in my head.

"Because you're my best friend! You're supposed to be the one person I can rely on, and instead you've just been lying to me." Tears swim in her eyes, remorse encompassing me all over again. "I don't care about Bryan, he's just a distraction and none the wiser. He figured I knew but just didn't want to bring it up and make things uncomfortable. I should have known you'd always protect her over me."

"Seriously?" My heart is pounding faster than I ever imagined it could, heat filling me from my head to my toes. "You're wrong, Bethany. It had nothing to do with that."

"Like I'll ever believe you," she guffaws, leaving me feeling like trash.

"I couldn't tell you without hurting you both. Either way I played it, everyone lost. I figured it was Anaya's truth to tell. I thought she would speak up eventually." My hands are blotching, my vision dotting, and I feel weak and restless at the same time. How did I let this go on for so long? Who was I kidding? I should have forced Anaya to speak up; I knew it would ruin us all eventually.

She nods her head, mouth pursed in disappointment. "Right." She shrugs, and then it's done, too late, and she's walking away.

Begrudgingly, I pick up a champagne flute a few minutes later and wait in a far off corner until the light show begins. Devin, of course, finds me just in time but does not bother me with interrogating questions. He simply waits until I'm ready to speak.

"How was it today with her?" I lift the champagne to my lips before offering him my glass. He takes it without question.

"Fine. She was quiet, also angry, understandably."

"I'm so stupid for thinking this had anything to do with Bryan. I should have known it was more about us than anything else." I sigh, wishing for a way to fix this all without scathing anyone else in the process.

The nighttime show begins, showering us in attractive sprouts of glowing water and tinny music. It is difficult not to enjoy, even in my current state.

"Hey, whatever they have going on is hard to get a read on, so I get it." Devin, always the root of reassurance, does his job well. Part of me relaxes against his strong frame while the rest of the crowd cheers at the ever changing lights.

"Who would have thought this trip would end up being a total bust?" I chuckle, but he puts his arm around my waist and leans in close.

"Well, I wouldn't say it was a *total* bust. I did get the girl, after all." He whispers, sending shivers up my spine.

"Yeah, yeah," I murmur gruffly, but when he turns to kiss me, I feel myself come back to life just some.

Thirteen

Our trip to the airport could not be any more off-putting. Our flight is delayed twice before we are finally put on a red-eye back to O-Town. Bethany refuses to speak to anyone who isn't Bryan or Devin, Devin feels bad speaking to Bethany without also being able to talk to me, and Anaya will not talk to anyone for fear of worsening the situation. Anyone who's seen us addresses us as a group of strangers who just happen to be sitting next to one another.

On the flight, I do my best to sleep, but my thoughts are warped by images of Bethany leaving our apartment, or worse, Bethany *and* Anaya leaving our apartment, and I find that I am on edge with no hopes of getting any reasonable amount of rest.

"Can't sleep?" Devin asks, voice gruff with sleep halfway through our flight. Contrarily, he's been able to catch quite some shut-eye.

"Not at all," I moan, willing myself to let my worries die so that I can at least check out from the rest of this trip.

"I can already tell you that you're getting way ahead of yourself. No one is happy right now, but you girls have been through too much to call it quits." Devin twists in his seat, eyes sleepy as he does his best to stay awake for me. "So let's flip this conversation."

"Really?" I chuckle miserably.

"Yeah, so let's see...Anywhere you want to travel to in the next year?" he prompts, and I'm so grateful to have his ridiculous antics at this moment that I hastily kiss him before thinking.

"I already told you I wanted to see the Alamo," I tease, batting my lashes.

"That kind of traveling doesn't count, Abby. We'd be visiting my family. Next!" His voice heightens jokingly and I grin. The thought of spending time with Devin's family unsettles me, but it isn't something we have to worry about right now. It may be something we *never* have to worry about, if this proves to be short-lived. I'm more intuitive than that though, nothing about this will be short.

"Jeez, you're a tough one. I don't know, I think I'd like to see mountains? Maybe the Rocky Mountains? Or Mount Rainier?" While the conversation feels farfetched, it is doing the trick of playing the ever distracting dialect.

"I'm down, but what about internationally?" Devin yawns, stretching his arms above his head.

"Okay, now I *know* this conversation isn't serious." My eyes roll without prior permission, but it doesn't deter Devin. He only winks.

"Never say never. Now, really, where would you go if you could?"

"Is this really a question?" I pout. "Every Disney park known to man. Hello! We are slaves to the Mouse, after all."

"Quick thinking, but which one? I will judge you based on your first choice." Devin's stare is grave but he struggles to keep his composure.

"Too much pressure," I giggle, running through a mental catalogue of known Disney locations.

"Be very careful, Abigail. The future of this relationship *and* friendship hang in the balance." he warns.

We ensue a stare off that lasts no more than ten seconds before we both break into fits of laughter.

"Doofus," I cluck my tongue. "I don't know, Shanghai? Their Pirates ride looks sick."

"If you'll look at that. A pirate for life, eh?" Devin nods his head accordingly, mentally jotting down notes on my response. "Not a bad one."

"What does that mean?" My brows furrow, but I know he's not telling.

"Nothing I'll ever tell," he shrugs, but I remind myself to touch back on that later. "Have you seen the Phantom Manor in Paris? Really cool Haunted Mansion concept."

"I haven't," I answer, proposing interest, and then Devin is pulling up a full ride-through for us to watch. From there on out, time flies. By the time we buckle up for landing, we've seen videos on just about every unique ride Paris, Shanghai, and Tokyo have to offer.

"I think I still stand by my choice of interest in Shanghai. They have StellaLou merch, you know. Priorities, am I right?" We deplane, welcoming the fresh, humid-filled Florida air. I never thought I'd miss it this much.

While it isn't widely known, I am a sucker for spending most of the hard earned money I scavenge from the Mouse (and my CM discount) on stuffed animals, specifically the ones with overly beady, adorable eyes. It is a personal problem I'm not too fond to admit to at twenty-three. Anyone who has seen my room knows I have an addiction, but I do my best to manage it, frequently swearing off any fluffy purchases for months. Did I cave in California? You guess.

"You have a problem, you know that?" Devin scuffles with a few Wishable plushes I made off with, lugging the small and outright adorable army under his arm.

"I rather not address it," I flush, squishing the cheek of a small Mickey, excited at the prospect of decorating my room with even more new friends. Is this what a mid-twenty life crisis looks like?

The rest of the gang shuffles in silence behind us, solemnly following our lead to the Uber pick-up.

My stomach begins to churn again at the thought of what will happen once we're all behind closed doors, but I choose to take Devin's word and assume that with time, most or all will be resolved.

In our SUV, the pin drop quiet is exasperating, and I see no option but to attempt to converse, not for lack of my own dismay. "I honestly really liked California. So, what's the final verdict? Disneyland or Disney World?" I add a small anxiety induced laugh to punctuate my words, but the oncoming mixed mumble that comes from everyone tells me that no one will be keeping on with any kind of conversation I try at.

If it's this hard now, what can I expect when we get back to the apartment? Should I start looking up new leases? What do

I do in the meantime? I can't handle the awkward tiptoeing for too long, it'll drive me crazy.

"Nice try," Devin nudges my shoulder when he notices just how put off I am by the lack of interaction.

"Thanks." The rest of the ride is masked in small, redundant questions made by our obviously uncomfortable driver. When we finally make it home, a medley of doubt and dread blossoms in my chest.

Inside, Devin helps me unpack in hushed whispers as we attempt to listen in on any other sort of conversation that might be going on across the hall. We're only gifted with drawn-out silence. We fill in the blanks with impromptu Disney trivia and talks of getting back to work in a days' time. While his distractions are more than welcome, I'm beginning to feel sorry for his overzealous attempts, and am about to tell him so when something strange happens.

"I got it?" Devin's breath leaves him, and I glance up from my newly assorted stuffed babies to see him glancing down at his phone, a mix of perplexity and excitement written on his face. "I got it!"

"Got what?" I tread carefully, my heart pounding in my ears.

"The engineering internship!" He rushes over to my side, picking me up and spinning me on my heels.

"What?" I squeal, hugging him fiercely. "That's amazing! When can you start?"

"Well, I have to accept the position before anything, and then there's training and all that other boring stuff, but I actually landed it! I can't believe it," we're laughing madly, momentarily forgetting all our current problems at hand.

I put my hands to his face, grinning wide. "Do you at least know what park you'll be at? You'd have a blast over in Pandora, I bet." The gears in my mind are turning at all the possible outcomes that can accompany his foot in the door: a stable, full-time job, a real shot at being an Imagineer, pay raises.

Slowly, his body tenses against mine. I get the feeling there's something that I'm missing, and I won't be happy to hear it.

"Well, I didn't want to jinx it, but while we were in California, Bethany's friend set me up with an interview. I didn't think much of it, but it's so hard to land one these days, so I went in not expecting much. It looks like I just got the luck of the draw." Devin's words make no sense, and all at once I know I've lost him. Of course, expecting anything I actually want for myself to last long-term was far-fetched. This is Disney, after all. No magic stays around forever. I've been stupid.

"So, not here. Not in Orlando." I speak slowly, careful not to reveal my true thoughts or trip over any words that will give me away.

"No, not here," he affirms, his face starting to drop in a way that makes me hate myself. "Anaheim."

"Anaheim," I repeat, at a lack of my own vernacular.

Our eyes lock and I am thankfully able to conjure up a smile that I convince myself is as genuine as can be. "I'm so proud of you." I say, the words not quite feeling my own, but true none the less. "Are you going to accept?" I ask, already knowing the answer.

"I think I have to," he shakes his head at me, willing me to understand, though I don't quite know how he sees I'm hurt if I'm trying so hard to hide it. "This might be my only chance for a while, Abby."

"You're absolutely right," I say, watching his thumb hover over his acceptance offer. The screen details that he'll be working with new extensions to Galaxy's Edge while shadowing veteran Imagineers on newer projects.

"But," he adds, "I won't take this if it's going to be a strain. I don't want this to ruin anything between us."

His words are sincere, making my eyes prick with emotion, but how, oh how, could I let this brilliant man put his life on hold for a girl who's been too blind to even give him the light of day. How could I keep him from something this grand?

With my heart in my throat, I take the phone from his hand and cradle it in my own. "You don't have to worry about any of that," I lie through my teeth, holding my breath as I do the deed for him, accepting his proposed position at the Disneyland Resort in Anaheim, California. His new home, his new life.

Without me.

"We'll be just fine," I hold him close, knowing that is the farthest from the truth. Nothing will be fine. This is the beginning of the end.

Fourteen

I was able to keep on a brave face for all the hours that Devin stayed behind, discussing possibilities of living arrangements, project proposals, and my joining him along for his week-long training that was to commence sometime within the next month. Ideally, equating to the fact that I have Christmas and New Year's with Devin before he's gone for good. I sleepwalked through it all, posing as the ever pleasant Abigail, nodding through grievances and grinning away my worries until I'd done it for so long that I believed it.

His letter noted that within the next three days, he'd receive a follow-up email with explicit details as to how the training process would be, when it would take place, and where to report. There was too much excitement on his face for me to do anything other than mirror his own enthusiasm, and even in the midst of my abrupt grief, I couldn't be the one to put a damper on the one thing he's been holding his breath on.

The moment he left, I felt my façade crumble into sharp shards of loss and defeat. Devin couldn't see it now, but none of this relationship would be permanent. It would only be a few months before we both agreed whatever this is can't be worth all the upkeep it entails, and then it would be over. A friend lost to time and space.

These are the thoughts that keep me up at night, questioning my judgment and wondering how I'm supposed to make it the next month without outright revealing to Devin that he may have very likely broken my heart before he's even been given the chance to try.

I have nothing to do but pace around my apartment, willing for some new awareness to present itself as the sole answer to all of my problems. I ache to speak to my friends but know there is nothing I can do to make them hear what I have to say now. Bethany refuses to listen to a word I have to say, and any word I utter to Anaya feels like an automatic bit of betrayal to Bethany. The newfound silence of the apartment brings an icy chill to my bones that I can't quite shake. Out on the balcony, I listen to the comforting disharmony of car engines, revving in the dead of night as they lull me to sleep in the Florida heat.

"I have to say, I always pegged myself as the most dramatic of us all, but you, my dear, have clearly been holding out in the theatrics department." Anaya's voice is the first I hear when I awake, scrunched up into a fetal position on our deck, sweat slick to my forehead. She plops down beside me, face dull.

"Would you believe it if I told you that I slept the whole night out here?" I say, doubtful myself of how I accomplished such a feat.

"You are a novelty," she plays, passing me a piping hot cup of coffee. Upon a deep breathe, the scent of blueberry hits my nose. My favorite.

"How does it feel to quit Instagram cold turkey?" I ask, eager to figure out most, if not all, of what is going on.

"I don't care about that right now, Abigail. I want Bethany to forgive me." Anaya blows over her cup. I take a hasty sip without caution. It only burns the roof of my mouth a tad.

"Same. Are you done trying to make a blog?" I continue, itching for answers.

"No, I'm not," she pauses before responding. It's evident she cares deeply about whatever she plans to put out there. I hurt for her having to put it all on hold, but I'm also aware it's our very own fault.

"Devin got a job offer in California. He'll be gone by the end of the month." The pain in my gut builds.

"What?" Anaya stops mid-coffee sip, her face blanching.

"Yeah," I shrug as if I haven't thought of every possible scenario in the last few painful hours since hearing the news.

"That's great for him, but you aren't happy about it, are you?" She treads carefully, dropping a sorry hand over my wrist.

"No, I'm not, but let's not tell him that." I say, moving my palm from under her grasp. Everything has gone tumbling in under a matter of seventy-two hours. I always figured that this magical life would be temporary for us some, that bits and pieces of us would come and go as time went on, but this is worse than I could have possibly imagined it.

"Guess it's just you and me."

"Lucky us." I gripe.

We spend the day moping within the confinements of our home, as Bethany flew the coop earlier than we could guess to head back to work. Making back for Pirates sounds like a plausible distraction, but Devin is currently there and I still haven't decided how I'm going to pull myself together and act normal when I see him again.

Anaya stays far, far away from her phone, but instead furiously types away at her laptop for a good portion of the day. It could just be some serious online shopping, or it could be something so much more. I wish I found myself undeterred in the face of trouble, but we are far from the same kind of person.

Fifteen

"How does Galaxy's Edge compare to the one we've got here?" Creepy James is back at it again upon my speedy return to Pirates. Oh, how I've come to miss the musty smell of this rundown place. Everything from the dimly candlelit halls to the overstated sound of rushing water, the laughs I exchange when crossing Devin's path, even the sight of managers just dropping in to check on me. Everything and everyone, aside from Creepy James.

Days have passed, and in the absence of a solid friendship foundation, I have found comfort in the voice of my inner monologue. Thoughts tumble between what I can do to speak normally to Devin and the sort of apology gifts I can snag for Bethany.

"James, I rather not ruin your sport." I grin smugly, not much for masking my true emotions today. It's my third day back on scene and each and every moment has dragged like a painfully awkward high school reunion.

"So, it's better," James sniffs, reaching up to reposition the glasses perched at the fine end of his nose. "*Or*, it's worse!"

With a hand on my hip, I dip my shoulder. "I'll never tell."

Guests shuffle past us as we kindly encourage them to get off the ride at a faster rate than they're accustomed to.

Just then, Devin approaches James slowly from behind, taking his deliberate time to creep (ha!) up on him.

I try my best to smile, but the look in his eyes tells me that I'm visibly off.

"James, it is time, you have been chosen." He taps him on the shoulder, handing over his new rotation and taking his place alongside me.

"I go on to a better place now." James turns to us both and we politely wait until he's out of earshot to laugh between directing guests.

"Enjoy your Christmas," I wave in mock jubilance, knowing that unlike most other cast members, I have been one of the few chosen to go on to a worse place, and by that I mean working tomorrow on Christmas Day.

"It's pretty sad that you know how to talk to him, you know." I grin, though my insides feel like they're slowly rotting.

"Have you been able to get rid of your Christmas shift yet?" Devin asks, always the model representation of a great cast member. He smiles wide enough that I can see the inside of his cheeks and continues to two-finger point while speaking to me through his teeth.

"No, and with less than twenty-four hours to bat, all hope has abandoned ship." I reply, my presentation much less of that of a great Disney cast member.

"I'll ask around," he bumps my shoulder. "Want to check out DAK after work?" A group of women eye us oddly as they pass by, probably as a result of our odd lingo.

DAK = Disney's Animal Kingdom.

"I wish," I nod, but my heart isn't in it. "Anaya wants us all to have dinner later tonight, though. You know, keeping up with traditions. Murdering each other at the dinner table. The likes."

"Are you feeling alright?" Devin asks, and something about the constant pressure of his questioning angers me. "You don't look like you've slept."

Another boat releases; we wait silently, smile and wave, encourage everyone to GTFO.

I turn the accusation back on him. "I'm not," I snort. "I'm not sleeping."

Instantly, I regret my words, but Devin is too focused on ensuring the guests have an enjoyable experience and I'm saved a few moments. "Exit to the left of your boat. Have a magical day!" One hand points in uniformity while the other wags a two-finger point. On the cast member rating scale I'd give him a ten. Today, I'm more along the lines of a four.

"Sorry, I'm just stressed. I didn't mean to snap." I put a hand to my forehead. The cast member running the mechanics of the ride behind her podium is clearly enjoying our little altercation, but this is Disney, and I'd be lying if I told you everyone and their supervisor didn't know Devin and I were now an item. Oh, and also all of Anaya's drama. I'd also be lying about that. Yes, they know. Yes, I am doing my best to fake ignorance.

"It's alright," he replies, but I can tell he wants to say more. Instead, I settle for the electric jolt of the brush of his hand against mine before the next incoming boat arrives.

Then, I'm being tapped on the arm by John, another tolerable cast member, who gives me my next assignment. I'm off to the tower and can breathe a sigh of relief knowing I won't have to explain myself for a while longer.

"See you tonight." I say, eyes on Devin after giving John a holiday-style hug.

"We did a great job," I nod at Bethany, regarding our decorative Stranger Things Christmas lights wall.

That afternoon, Anaya, Beth and I worked in peaceful harmony to put together the most festive apartment we've ever laid our eyes on. Though we aren't much of a group of friends anymore, we have plenty of acquaintances outside of our intricate circle that are more than thrilled to attend our holiday bash. Many included Anaya's local Instagram friends who have been surprisingly supportive of the entire situation, but whether they're coming for dinner or a show is up in the air.

"Mhm," Beth gives me a small smile, but with it being our first direct conversation in about a week, I wouldn't call it progress.

"How are you feeling?" I blurt, brave among the throng of people I don't associate with, giving me no other choice but to try to repair what matters most during the season of giving.

"Not great, Abigail," she tilts her shoulder defensively, but as she scoots in closer to ward off any wandering ears, I feel hopeful.

"I know what you mean," I smile sadly, watching as Bryan walks in, accompanied by Devin and the rest of their dweeb friends. Bethany's eyebrows raise in question, but I have nothing else to say.

"You have Devin, it can't be so bad." She whispers. I shake my head.

"He's leaving, Beth." I monotone, willing it to not be true. My eyes follow his greetings to old friends across the room as they bid him farewell and wish him good luck.

It's painful to watch, but I can't force myself to look away. Soon enough, it'll be my turn, and I'll have to know just how to do it.

"It's not forever. Plus, he'll be back after training for a little while." Bethany's words are an afterthought, presenting themselves too late after I'd spent all afternoon making my final decision.

The prospect of us was great, no, it was fantastic, cosmic, but also, apparently, unrealistic and unideal. How long would I be able to wring myself thin with a boyfriend that's thousands of miles away without it tarnishing whatever is left of our friendship, as well? It's not right, not for him, and not for me. There's no reason I should hold him back from a future so close to the Walt Disney Studios. There are too many doors he hasn't even thought to touch and all I'm doing is preventing his full potential from shining. So, this is it. I won't be a hindrance. I'll go on with this little odd life that I enjoy dedicating to the Mouse, and he will do so, too. Far, far away from me.

"It's not enough," I say, the words ringing too true once I've said them out loud. I'll be sure to save them for later. The way that my not-so-best friend looks at me now makes me want to question my values, but I can't let one person deter me from what's ultimately inevitable.

She looks to swallow her words and comes up short. "Okay," she says, sipping from her cider and looking in the direction of Bryan, who will be in our vicinity in the next few moments.

"I miss you, you know." I pull her close for a hug before she can protest, and while she's stiff in my grasp, she doesn't push me away. "I'm sorry I hurt you." I whisper and then leave her to enjoy the rest of her night without worries of traitorous friends.

I fill the next few hours with conversation between Anaya's old Instagram friends and other cast members who never really left after their College Program. The excitement in the air is palpable and everyone is practically glowing with appreciation. In the absence of parents and siblings, we've all grown to lean on each other. I'm thankful to have so many people I can trust, and hope that some of them will be of service after I self-sabotage in the next few hours.

Figuring I can only go so long avoiding Devin before he begins to question whether that's exactly what I'm doing, I find him self-serving at the Christmas Cheer bar we put together with a whole liter of vodka and funky fruit juices.

"You're holding the jug funny," I clear my throat, watching him use a single hand to tilt the juice in a pretty risky fashion.

"Thanks for noticing." He caps the lid, taking a sip before passing the drink over to me. "I like what you did to the place."

"It was a last ditch effort. Sorry that I couldn't make it to the park with you." I apologize, knowing I'm actually extremely thankful for the excuse to pass up hurting myself any more than I already have to.

"Next time," he smiles, his face carefree as he twirls me underneath the Christmas tree to the beat of "Last Christmas." The ache in my chest is a dull note against the rest of everything else my soul is mulling over.

"Sure," I laugh as if it's that easy, eager to turn my thoughts elsewhere. "Someone snatched my shift last minute, apparently, so looks like I'm free for Christmas."

"Nice!" he sways me slowly and I can feel a larger part of the room's eyes on us.

Anaya pops her face in between us. "Don't you miss my interruptions? You guys are too adorable. It makes me want to hurl."

"I *definitely* miss them," I escape from his grasp, throwing my arms around her neck.

"Glad to hear it. We're going to start party games in a few minutes, so gather your bearings now." She flicks my nose.

"Yes, Mom," Devin rolls his eyes, taking me by the arm and pulling me outside. I shoot Anaya a look that should translate to something along the lines of SAVE ME but her brows only knit in confusion. I mentioned I've kept my little revelation to myself, yes?

Outside, the air is humid, giving no sign that Ol' Saint Nick will be on his merry little way tonight. The sound of drunk laughter and festive tunes ring out between the silence. I could break the news to him now and save us the next week's heartbreak, or I could continue to spare him in place of my suffering. Either way, we all lose.

"I think I found a place," Devin starts, equally as edgy. "Have I shown you?"

"You leave in two days." I say dazedly.

"I know, Abby, but I'll be back for New Year's." He reaches a hand out to me, but I shy away from his touch, surprised at my own body's response. I figured, at least, I'd be able to hold out awhile longer.

"And then gone again." My words are dry, tongue sticking to the roof of my mouth, maybe to prevent whatever disaster I'm about to bring about next.

"Only for a few months." His mouth frowns. "I'll come back and visit and then we can—" He's reaching, I know it. We're both idiots for suspecting something like this job is temporary.

"For how long, Dev? Am I supposed to sit here waiting for you while you're making your life happen?" I step back from him, elongating the distance between us so that I hopefully don't have to explain myself in full detail.

"Where's this coming from?" His voice is getting smaller by the second, and I despise it. My heart feels like it's ready to crack open before what comes next.

And then it does.

"I think I preferred being your friend." My eyes close against the words, bracing for the astronomical impact of full on heart failure.

"That's a lie."

My eyes snap open. His bore into mine, daring me to contradict him. While the fib is weak, it's all I have. I can't take back what I say next.

"It's not," I shrug. "I don't think I feel about you the way I thought I did."

"That's rich, Abigail." He looks like he's been shot but hides it better than I do. Without reaching my hand up to check, I know my face is tear-stained. "Should have known you'd back out of this the moment things get tough."

"What's that supposed to mean?" I reckon, the pain in my core enveloping everything else that works together to conduct my functioning.

"Whatever you want it to," he shrugs. I know he's given up and I have nothing else to say. Instead, I wrap my arms around my shoulders and give him a remorseful smile. With a shake of his head, he leaves me in the heat.

The beat drumming in my chest tells me I'm still alive but just barely. I allow myself a few minutes of private recollection, telling myself that the worst is over and eventually I'll heal, but the thoughts feel empty and my bones are hollow. I'm a walking shell.

"There you are!" Anaya bellows when I reenter the room, beckoning me to the hefty circle that's formed in the middle of our living room.

I drop down next to Bethany, who eyes me warily as I smile beside her, careful to keep up with the festivities and not give myself away.

She knows me better than I know myself some days and reaches behind me to rub small circles on my back as an honorary game of Truth of Dare unfolds.

I listen in on people who've eaten from the ice cream cart on the job, attraction workers that have gotten selfies with celebrities, and how Snoop Dogg likes his chicken nuggets when he visits Pinocchio's Village Haus. All the while, my eyes are on him, halfway across the room. The way his jaw tenses tells me I've ruined his night. It would bring him joy to know that I've also ruined my own. His hand clenches, unfurls, wriggles, clenches again. All of me wants to go to him and fix this. Every bit.

And then his head whips, catches me watching him, wanting him.

"Truth or dare?" His lips move but the room is quiet as all eyes go to me. A few boys whistle and other girls titter with laughter. Bethany's hand on me stills.

"Uh," the words choke me, my cheeks burning red as I clear my throat. "Truth," I say with finality. Regardless of what he might ask, I've always been afraid of a good dare. Another problem to add to my psyche.

His eyes are questioning me but I can't hold them with my own. My eyes involuntarily flit to Anaya, who has better intuition than I give her credit for and has definitely picked up on what's going on here.

"What's the worst thing that's happened to you as a cast member?" he fishes, and there are lots of technicalities I'd like to take into consideration.

On the job or off? If off, we are by far talking about five minutes ago when I outright lied to you! Remember that? Sorry, I guess.

"The one time I got a drink thrown at me." I say, matter-of-factly. It is my go-to ice breaker.

"Epcot?" The corner of Devin's lips curl.

"Yes," I say, and the way Bethany's fingers are tapping on me lets me know there will be questions. "I let a heavily-intoxicated man know that the keg was out—lie!—and he proceeded to throw his Italian margarita at me."

I told you I'd get to that story.

Sixteen

The next morning feels worse than any hangover I've ever had and it has nothing to do with alcohol.

"Merry Christmas," I whisper to the presents under the tree, obligatory coffee cup at hand. I leave another two out for my lovely roommates, who any minute now I'm sure will be coming out of their rooms to announce the aforementioned: it's Christmas. Feeling impatient myself and a little bit lonely, I begin to call throughout the apartment.

"Let's go, ladies!" I knock on Anaya's door before opening. "If you're lucky, Santa's been—Hello?" I pause, hand against the door. Bethany and Anaya appear to be sitting together, smiling for a selfie. "Is this a Christmas miracle?" I blurt.

Anaya sticks her tongue out, eyes bulging. "Looks like we're being joined by the final gal in our trio." She shifts her phone screen at me, but I'm frozen. "Hi!" I say once my bearings have been gathered. Anaya is quick to recover, taking back the attention.

"We've been holding out on you but talked it over and decided that it's been long enough. We're ready to discuss what went on. But firstly, I'm going to start by saying that after this video, this account will be deactivated for good and I'll be taking my talents over to the Insta handle on my bio." Anaya's voice has taken on its Instagram-official voice. Bethany is nodding behind her.

What?

"*What!*" I almost growl, hopping onto the bed behind Bethany.

"We also want to let everyone know there is no bad blood between us. Everyone in this room was aware of the photos, and we're friends before anything else. Whoever was trying to mess with that is out of luck, because nothing has changed between us. Point blank: those photos were taken before Bryan and I got close. They mean absolutely nothing to me. Whoever released them was looking to gripe at something that is completely irrelevant, so to whoever you are, try harder next time."

We're lying to the internet? Holy.

"Yep!" I tilt my head with sass, wondering what I've missed and if this is really an entire elaborate hoax, or, you know, just a little one.

Anaya grins at me in the monitor. "So, now that you have it, we'll make some time for questions before signing off for good. And, remember, this isn't goodbye. You'll be able to catch new photos and blog posts over at the handle on my bio, so make sure you check that out."

Lie or not, this is genius. Anaya is broadcasting her new Instagram handle and shutting down the toxic one. The incident's reputation won't follow her, and we'll all be able to start fresh. Maybe.

We wait excitedly as the inpouring questions and notions of support pile up. The comments are coming in too fast for me to catch onto a single one, but Bethany and Anaya don't bat a lash.

Bethany: "Yes! I will definitely be coming out in posts on Anaya's new page."

Anaya: "Those photos rocked our friendship in the sense that we felt attacked, and almost betrayed, really, by our online family, but we're fine. Nothing has changed between us. If anything we're stronger."

Okay, sureeeeeee.

Me, finally: "I don't really know how I didn't get dragged into this, but as most of you know, I've been subjected to other online scandals in the past. I guess whoever dug this up decided to give me a break. Ha!"

Accordingly, comments as to whether Devin and I are going strong, if we're officially dating, how we met, and where he is, come in.

Anaya and Bethany giggle, jabbing me. "Looks like they have lots of questions for you." I find it alarming how well they're able to act for this little video.

I bite my lip, uncertain of what to say and not feeling up to the charade, but then Bethany and Anaya are waving. "Hi, Devin! Thanks!"

My eyes drift to his comment. He's congratulated us on our brisk return to the Disney community and wishes us well going forward.

"Merry Christmas," I respond with a small smile, and the hiccup only goes noticed by Anaya, who tenses before quickly recovering.

Merry Christmas, Abigail.

I'm quiet the majority of the rest of our live video. We all grow a bit teary-eyed when Anaya concludes, readying herself to disable an account that she's put years of effort into. We help her to delete every post she's ever made on the account, leaving only one detailing that she's moved her platform to a new media handle.

When it's over, she releases a large breath that voices just how uncertain she is about this all. A quick peek at the new platform tells me she's already brought over 7K worth of people, but that is a grain of sand next to the numbers she once possessed. Either way, the change is necessary, and I'll do whatever she needs to help her grow her presence again.

"Thank you, Bethany. You really didn't have to do that but I'm so grateful you did." Anaya puts a hand on Bethany's arm, but her face is less than welcoming.

"Yep," she smiles through her teeth.

"It was all fake? For the video?" I deadpan, angered that even on Christmas we can't expect to be civil. Anaya looks ashamed.

"It needed to be done to save her reputation. I'm still angry, but we're working on it." Bethany sighs, a hand to her face.

"Really?" I ask hopefully, adding before they can answer. "I made us coffee, if you wanted to go out and open gifts."

They both nod kindly. I'm certain they're only putting on brave faces for me, and I'm willing to ignore it if it means keeping at least some of my sanity.

"Speaking of lies," Bethany treads, looping an arm through my own. "What was that all about?"

"I don't know what you mean," I noticeably deflate.

"Ha! Okay, Merry Christmas, Abigail! You only get your

present when you dish out the goods!" Anaya chimes in behind us, always the instigator.

"Where should I start?" I sip cryptically.

"The beginning, of course."

"Merry Christmas, Bryan!" I hug him jubilantly, high on the thrill of my new motto of loving anyone and everyone on this Christmas day. Inevitably, though, I wait for the person who should come after him to greet me, but they're nowhere to be found. "Where's Devin?" I try my best to sound disinterested, but I probably should have given up this charade ages ago.

"Working." Bryan shrugs, wrapping Bethany in a loose hug. I need to remind myself to ask what's going on *there*.

"What? How? We just spoke yesterday. He had today off. I'm the one that..." I drift off, realization dawning on me that it was no accident. Approximately an hour and a half later, after a car ride, monorail transport, and detailed walk, I'm given the opportunity to ask my questions when we smuggle our way into the backstage break room.

"You're the one who picked up my shift." I point to Devin, arms crossed before him. The idea that he took my shift before our argument, all so I could spend the day with my friends, has added painstaking fuel to the fire. He leaves tomorrow. I should be the one in my Pirates costume.

"It's Christmas, woman. This is how you say hello?" His hands are in his pockets, chest curved inward in a protective stance despite his words. The air between us is taut with the words I said the night before.

I reach out to pull him in for a bear hug before I can think better of it. "Thank you," I whisper close to his ear. "And Merry Christmas."

"Same to you, Abs." He squeezes me tight, holding me longer than I should let him, and when we break away, I have to blink away the thought of any tears revealing themselves.

We exchange our presents, gifting Disney gift cards and knickknacks we've acquired through numerous shopping trips to Disney Springs, acting the picture perfect image of cast member friends. Even Bethany and Anaya do their best to act as if the argument is something behind them. I hold onto

Devin's gift, wondering if I should consider avoiding digging the knife into his heart. As we continue to unwrap memorabilia, I start to think that my present isn't as great as I thought it was. In fact, it feels ridiculous.

"How are you feeling?" Devin whispers, dissipating my thoughts. His hand on my back brings me so back to reality it's deathly. What would I do to reverse everything I said yesterday and just suffer in silence so that I could have bits and pieces of him for as long as I can?

Horrible.

"I'm okay," I smile through the pain, adjusting my Mickey Santa hat. I wish I knew how to push away from his touch.

"You're a terrible liar," he brushes his thumb along my waist and I clear my throat. His usual spunk is back, but there's no trace of a smile on his face. My cheeks beat red.

"I got you something," I say, knowing it's my only escape. "It's really nothing. I thought it would be nice. I see now that it really isn't all that great. It's actually pretty stupid." I blabber, hating myself. I'm supposed to be convincing him that my decision was final and I have no regrets. Nice try, Abigail.

Now, his hand does move and I'm able to breathe a sigh of relief.

"I'm sure I'll love it." He nods at the box I'm holding onto for dear life. "Your present will have to wait till I get back, though. I haven't gotten around to wrapping it up just yet."

"Sure," I say, handing over the medium-sized container adorned in pizza gift wrap.

Carefully, Devin undoes the presentation, working the paper in certain angles as not to rip anything unnecessarily. My heart drums in my chest as he gets closer and closer to opening it. Our friends wait around us quietly as he goes through the motions. Finally, he is opening a titanium bin, rattling its insides metallically. My eyes flit between him and the other cast members filing into the room. They give me a greeting but don't approach our party, as many of them are eager to call their loved ones or enjoy the holiday in solitude.

He glances inside, shuffling between bits of screws, metal sheets, miniature gears and other scraps of metal I thought might be of use.

"It's some spare parts," I supply, unsure that he's figured out what exactly I wanted to do for him this Christmas. "I thought that, I don't know, some of the things in there might be useful for you to make something cool out of."

"This is awesome!" Devin laughs, grinning childishly.

"I was trying to be thoughtful. I hope you like it." I fumble with the ruffles on my little red Christmas tree skirt, and the rest of the group around us shifts into their own conversations.

"I love it, I do, really," he says, and I know that he means it. My eyes travel up his face to finally meet his eyes. There is too much in them to decipher for a broken heart, so I only watch him, waiting to see who will be the first to break.

"We have a lunch reservation to make!" Bethany reminds everyone before either of us can prove the weak link, and then Devin is smiling, hugging us all goodbye.

"I'll see you when I get back," he tells me.

"Oh, you aren't going to meet up with us later? We'll probably hop over to Epcot tonight." The hope in my voice is unmistakable, even to me.

He shakes his head and I accept that I've caused this. "Too much to pack, but we'll do something fun next week."

"Sure." I agree, telling myself it's just a formality.

"I'm stuffed!" Anaya belches loud enough for the neighbors to hear when we return from dinner at Le Cellier, falling onto the couch no less theatrically.

Bethany has done no more than answer her questions with the utmost civility all day, but she can't hide the smile that forms on her mouth as she comes in trailing behind her.

I curl into a ball on our love seat, picking up the tray of cookies that have been left out since the morning. "Can't go the night without eating some of Santa's leftover cookies," I pick up one myself, disappointed to find that it's stale.

"Those have been out since this morning," Bethany laughs, but she goes on to pour us glasses of milk in the kitchen.

Anaya reaches for the cookies over her head. "Poor Santa," she frowns, plopping bits of the morsel into her mouth.

"So, am I allowed to say that today was interesting?" Bethany rounds the corner with a tray of sugar-rimmed milk glasses.

"How's your Instagram looking?" My head whips at Anaya, but both girls laugh.

"Not bad, I'm already up a few thousand followers. The ones that care will follow, the rest are of no use to me." Anaya raises her device, showing me her fast-growing profile. "Here, let's make a quick Christmas post."

We come close behind her and pose with our milk and cookies. She posts the photo, wishing everyone a fruitful holiday season but seldom else. Maybe, just maybe, this incident has been good for Anaya. With the way things are going, it seems to me that she's a lot more focused on what's in front of her as opposed to anything going on online.

Hoping to keep the peace between us, I pipe up. "What are our highlights of the day?"

The girls spend a few seconds munching and considering. Anaya is the first to inquire. "For me it's a solid tie between the face you made when the waiter at Le Cellier accidentally brought you the fish and when Bryan tripped over that stroller and landed on some big guy."

Bethany is laughing, finger pointed at me. "Okay, in my defense, it didn't look bad. I was just expecting my poutine! Fish is not poutine, guys." My words are barely heard over Bethany coming to her own realization.

"You know I'm a sucker for drama and occasional romance." She teases. "So, obviously the whole spare parts thing was adorable to me."

"Glad you enjoyed that fun at my expense." I raise my milk glass. "I personally loved making that video with you guys this morning. I miss the three of us together." The girls are silent, eyes wandering to inanimate objects but never to each other. "You guys are my family." I try to keep my emotions at bay but my voice is scratchy.

Bethany sighs and Anaya looks near tears. "We're working on it." Bethany comes over to me, wrapping me in her arms. "Promise."

"Good," I nod against her. "I'm sorry, again."

"Stop apologizing," she shushes me. "We need to figure out what kind of havoc we plan to make come New Year's."

"Leave it to me." Anaya winks. Always the mastermind.

Seventeen

"I could seriously go for a Dole Whip right about now." Jessica, who I haven't seen since our Ramona G. fiasco, nods at a guest who walks through the line, ravenously licking at her yellow-tinged spoon, a plump sorbet in her other hand. It's mildly repulsive, but I'm not supposed to have thoughts like that on the job.

I turn on my heel so the guests can't see me pull a face. "She's looking to marry it, I think."

Jessica holds back a laugh. "Wouldn't last that long," she clucks her tongue, and glancing over my shoulder, I notice it's already gone, a whole minute, maybe, later.

"How did she do that?" I gape in awe, slipping off my sunglasses to really take in the scene. The magic of Disney astounds me every day.

"Gotta keep my secrets, but I wish you witnessed what I just did. I'm going to have to religiously cleanse myself when I get home now." Jessica is definitely on my list of favorable Pirates coworkers, as she never offers anything short of a good laugh. She may be one of the more slack crewmates, but no one really enjoys the company of an uptight cast member and that's the truth.

A snort involuntarily escapes me, sending me into rocking fits of laughter that few guests question as they pass us by.

"Don't mind her, she stole Captain Jack's rum!" Jessica assures those that do look at us as though we're incapable of telling people to follow the person in front of them.

"You let me know where I can find it, then!" An older father pats me on the back and we share a hearty laugh.

Once I've calmed down enough to appear sensible, I smile appreciatively. "Thanks for that. I needed a good laugh." Jessica is one of the few people at work who has yet to ask me about He Who Must Not Be Named. It's emotionally exhausting to convince yourself you'll be fine while also subjecting yourself to insistent reminders of the one thing you're trying to take your mind off.

"Just doing my job, argh!" Jessica jumps in phony excitement, but we're both able to maintain our charade for the rest of our shift together, only cracking inappropriate jokes when the guests aren't close enough to hear us commenting on their suspicious smelling water bottles.

The Orlando gods have blessed us with reasonably cool weather today, the only hint that it is December and still not July in Florida, but the thought of walking through the heat of the underground tunnel at the end of my shift in a few hours has me nauseas. While all other parks keep their backstage shenanigans above ground, the rest of us struggle in hot and sweaty metal corridors at the start and finish of every day.

Just as I'm wondering if there is some way I can alternatively escape by changing my clothes and heading to Tommorrowland for a cream cheese pretzel, a familiar face comes into view.

"Hey there, Abigail! How are you doing today?" A voice much too chipper for me to compute is shouting in my face and I blink dubiously behind my well-tinted sunglasses (there's a reason I sport them almost every day). My mind wraps around the fact that Bethany is standing before me in her Guest Relations attire. I'll never get over the fact that their costumes obviously reign supreme over any other on Disney property.

"Bethany...hi! I'm doing great, how about you?" I pick up quick, offering her a hand to shake and knowing without glancing behind her that we have a few guests that have paid premium to personally be shown around the park.

"Feeling fantastic! I was just stopping by to take my friends here on Pirates." Bethany splays her palm out wide, smile tight as she motions behind her at a man and woman that are waiting for my approval with patient smiles.

Jessica is equally quick on her feet. "Hi there, ya'll! Ready for some fun?"

But I am transfixed, because I know this guy. I *know* this guy.

He's in his mid-thirties, broodingly attractive with light eyes and looking at me like a well-versed super hero.

That face...wait, that smile. Holy.

"I..." I blank behind my shades, searching for the right words to say to the guy who I have seen in more films than I can count. Bethany is biting her lip, pleased with how star struck I suddenly am. "I can walk you right up to the front. How's about that for some Disney magic?" I regain minimal thought processes, turning and leading the way before I can see the party make questioning glances at one another.

"Having a nice shift?" Bethany saddles up next to me in the dark corridor, practiced in the art of keeping her cool around enviously attractive males that are tied to the Disney Company one way or another. This, though? Is a whole other level. He's an Avenger!

"Um," I work to catch my breath, itching to whip around and let him know I love every movie he's ever done, especially, you know, the savior of our planet ones, but not feeling confident enough to risk my job.

"It's fine, save your words. He's very nice." She pats my back, and while I believe her, I want to know who the beautiful woman he's with is! *I wish I could ask right now. Jeez. I'm a sucker for theatrics. Why?*

I spend the rest of the brief walk to the loading dock wondering what I can say that can get all the emotions I feel for him across without jeopardizing my status as a pirate, coming up with very few things.

"Alright, here we are, folks." I turn, ushering them into the first row. As their boat arrives, I desperately take out a hand for Bethany to shake. "Have a great day!" I turn to the lady he's chosen to grace his presence with and do the same, and then there's him. Watching me. Smiling. Heaven help me.

"Thanks for saving the world, Cap!" I bellow, nearly losing my bearings. His hand is firm in mine, grip tight.

"Anytime, Abigail." He nods, taking on the persona of his fictional superhero. My mouth is still hanging open once the boat has taken off and left me back in my mundane life.

"Was that just—" James is navigating the mechanics, but I am speechless and can only nod. Best work day ever.

The rest of my shift passes surprisingly fast thanks to my mental replay of the hottest superhero ever calling me by my name, and Jessica, who is all too eager for me to repeat the story to any other crew member that crosses our path.

"How do you feel about cream cheese pretzels?" I propose to Jessica as we clock out and head for our lockers.

"I am partial to them, why do you ask?"

"I don't want to go home just yet." I shrug, and she does too.

"So, let's get out there then." She smiles, and while she's been less than vocal about it, I know she feels just a bit sorry for me. It's alright, though. I feel a bit sorry for myself, too.

"I really do think we can continue to tell this story for the rest of our Pirates days." Jessica laughs over the dole whip she finally got around to, though I don't know how she still wanted to touch anything like that after watching its scientific birth unfold before her. No celebrity interaction can erase what I didn't see and can only imagine in my head.

"You're not wrong." I laugh, having settled for popcorn as opposed to a cream cheese pretzel, knowing full well I'll probably end up eating both. I have little to no control around Disney food. This company pays me only for me to gladly give the corporate monster back its money.

A small ache in my chest reminds me that outside of this park I have a real, fully functioning life that requires my attention. Everything in here may look sparkling new and perfect, but everything outside it is anything but. Realistically, I knew that this is what drew me to the parks in the first place, the fabrication, the idea that nothing could ever go wrong.

"What are you thinking about?" Jessica probes.

"This month has really been a disaster," I nod towards her, considering the fact that rum infused dole whip is not gross and could actually be really helpful right about now.

"It'll get better. Look at today!" Jessica is a great hype woman. I make a note to invite her out more often. Bethany and Anaya would love her.

"Did you see the way he smiled at us? I felt so special. How lame am I?" I roll my eyes, wishing I could tell Devin all about it. He's more of a DC kind of guy but is still a big fan.

"I mean, I'm currently fantasizing about having his children, so..." Jessica trails off, and again we're laughing as if nothing is wrong and Disney is the only world that exists and matters.

I know better than to put my tail between my legs, but take my phone from my pocket and type away a message regardless. We're still friends, after all, aren't we?

You'll never guess who came through the ride today...

I wait a few minutes, my screen lit hopefully before it dawns on me that he won't be responding any time soon or possibly any time at all.

"I'm sure he's busy." Jessica notices the way my hands drum our Adventureland table impatiently, but there's nothing promising about her voice.

"Why do I feel like this is all you've been talking about all day?" Anaya barely looks my way as I recount today's exciting events.

"Well, I haven't *not* been talking about it." I refute, feeling less shameful than I should after banking off this story.

She chuckles, but her fingertips continue to heatedly type away on her laptop. "What do you recommend someone does on a rainy day at Disney?"

"Hmmm," I say before snapping my fingers. "Shopping at Disney Springs is probably my first go-to."

"Eh," Anaya tilts her head to the side, doubtfully typing.

"Most of Epcot's pavilions have indoor areas, and you don't have to worry about rides closing, so there's that. Also, you know, you could just get wet and enjoy minimal crowds."

"Better," Anaya nods, impressed a bit more but just barely.

"I'm no expert, you know me, rain is water." I laugh. "How are you and Bethany doing?"

Anaya is quiet, and for a moment I think she hasn't heard me, but then she pushes her laptop to the side. "Not great. She's barely said a word to me since Christmas."

"That's expected." I shrug, offering little else.

"Yeah," she nods, flopping onto her back and raising her hands to her forehead. "I actually have a Mickey's Very Merry Christmas Party coming up tomorrow. You wanna come with? I have a plus one."

"Sure," I agree, but a thought tells me I have a better idea.

Eighteen

"Did you want to go to a Christmas party tonight?" I ask Bethany the following morning when her eyes are tired with holiday work exhaust. "I was going to surprise Devin with tickets but obviously that didn't work out, so now I'm stuck with an extra." I add for good measure, fanning my neck with the ticket.

She watches me questioningly, deciding whether she's ready to let me back into her life just yet. We've been more amicable these last few days, so I'm not too worried about our relationship. It'll get taken care of. I care more about Anaya and her right now. They're the priority, and I'm willing to bet there are few ways to get them into the same room that doesn't involve such bribery.

"Okay." She agrees after a few painstaking moments, and I can't help the grin that finds its way to my face.

I plan the rest of my day away from the apartment, telling Bethany I'll meet her at Magic Kingdom at dusk once her shift is over, and feeding an eerily similar line to Anaya, hoping for whatever reason their paths won't cross before then and soil my plan.

Instead, I decide that a solo day at Animal Kingdom is in the cards for me. I could easily invite any single friend to join me, but lately the empty feeling I'm blessed with upon having company is starting to wear thin.

Initially, I wander aimlessly around Discovery Island, drinking coffee, window shopping, and purely distracting myself from any other stress, but I find that the more I try to immerse myself in the lie, the more I wonder how Devin is doing in California and why he's suddenly too busy to respond to one small message.

I take to science to solve it, snapping a quick photo of myself with the Tree of Life and posting it online. Within a few hours, I'd know if I was being ignored or if I just wasn't an active priority. For some time I think I figured that I was above the online predatory that Anaya practices on a daily basis, but now I know that very few of us are and that the internet is quite convenient. How else would we know who is worth dating?

In the meantime, I go through the motions of riding, eating, and leisurely strolling. It feels good to casually do something that we take for granted so often, but it be a lie to say that I'm wholly content being alone at the park. Don't get me wrong, there's nothing like it, but I'd probably be much happier about it if everything in my life hadn't recently hit the fan.

I miss being able to tell people irrelevant fun facts about the park after having been deployed to Dinosaur for less than a week and discovering other hidden details and paths of the park I haven't before. Cast member parkhopping is quite the experience, and there's always something interesting to share. While more than anything, Devin was the one delivering the relevant information, it wasn't just him I missed. It was a lot more than that. As it turns out, Disney isn't half as magical without my friends.

The next few hours are spent moping and enjoying sinful foods that I have every right to eat in this condition. What else are buffalo chicken chips for than heartbreak?

"Yep, I'm on my way. Just wait for me outside of the fire station. I'll be there soon." I smile through my teeth, fibbing in a bathroom at 6:45PM, thankful that Bethany is not suspicious.

Meanwhile, Anaya has already texted me she'll be a few minutes early and just happens to be standing outside of the fire station. Here's to hoping no one gets killed tonight. It would make a fairly horrible newspaper headline.

In the moments leading up to seven, I'm extremely anxious and choose to busy myself by checking on who has seen my previous Instagram stories. No surprise, Devin has seen every one and has not replied to any or bothered to text me back.

Feeling otherwise hopeless, I do something I never thought I'd have to in a million years.

"Hello?" Bryan picks up on the second ring.

"Bryan," I hold my breath. "Are you busy tonight?"

"Are you girls up to something?" He laughs, assuming that of course I'd never want to do anything absolutely ever with just him and I. Kudos to his spot-on intuition.

"Not at all. I'm actually alone." I say, feeling the slightest bit pathetic. This must be what rock bottom feels like.

"Okay," he recovers quickly, acting like this is a pretty normal inquiry. "What do you want to do?" As he says this, my phone beeps, alerting me that Bethany is calling. I ignore the notification.

"I don't know." I shrug, tapping my fingers against my thigh. "I could eat, I guess."

"Me, too. I'll meet you at Epcot in half an hour."

"This is unexpectedly pretty great." I speak through my munching on lamb at Spice Road Table in the Morocco pavilion, my phone still going off every few minutes as Bethany and Anaya both have many words they'd like to share with me. Unfortunately, they'll have to share them with each other. I've opted to erase the multiple voicemails they've left, as well.

When Bryan had insisted we meet here for a bite to eat, I'd been skeptical but was also in no position to play the spoiled brat. He'd been doing me a favor enough as it is just agreeing to be seen with me.

"Told you," Bryan mumbles over his own meal, a fish of sort that I am mentally considering may be better than my own. We'd had little much to talk about aside from the menu.

"Have you been working this week?" I ask now, thinking this is as close to normal conversation as we'll ever probably get.

"Not at all, I've lucked out." Bryan grins and I laugh.

"I'm jealous, I feel like I haven't stopped since we've gotten back from California." Though, that is by choice, I want to add. He gives me a look that says as much.

"How are Bethany and Anaya these days?" He switches conversation instead, thankfully.

"Getting around to it." I shrug. "I'm hoping it won't be long before things go back to normal. Mostly, at least, I mean."

I shut my eyes, hating my lack of social awareness being so easily revealed.

"I'm sure. She forgives you guys, you know. It's just a sucky situation." Bryan surprisingly opens up and I take it as my one moment to ask the questions I want to.

"How are you and Bethany?" The question is broad and it may not give me an idea of the nature of their relationship, but if it's something neither has wanted to share with us then I have no choice but to respect the decision.

"We're okay. I feel bad about this whole thing. I didn't think it was going to come up. I figured, you know, it was just something we didn't want to talk about. I didn't know she was in the dark." Bryan's cheeks take on a rose shade that gives the allusion that he may actually be charming.

"Yeah," I say, guilt washing over me. Once again, I find myself the root of my own problems.

"It isn't your fault, you know." Bryan kicks me under the table, sending my brain into a momentary mush.

"That's a lie," I laugh. "I should have said something."

"It really isn't. How were you supposed to say something?" He shakes his head, eyes squinted. "Anaya would have hated you. She's the one who put you in this situation, Abigail." He's echoing thoughts I've had recently but have been too afraid to voice. How could I put the blame on my other best friend?

"I'm very capable of making my own decisions. I could have easily avoided this." I shrug, not wanting to think that I'm associated in this altercation only by being an unwilling accomplice.

"Maybe, but then Anaya would have hated you, and so would have Bethany. You couldn't win. And I'm willing to bet you didn't say anything until now solely because Anaya begged you."

"I—" I start, but when I do, I have nowhere to finish. Bryan raises his brows at me, waiting. He doesn't look as though he wants to be right, but he is.

"Don't beat yourself up about it." He tilts his head, getting back to eating. "You only did what you could."

I want to say more, but part of me, no, most all of me, knows that he's right. I haven't wanted to put the blame on any other person involved, but the truth was that I felt a sense of loyalty to both friends, and I believed that with time Anaya would come clean and admit that I had only been quiet because she'd begged me. And part of me despises her for that, for choosing not to say something, for staying quiet for so long, and for taking my choice away from me. But I still don't want to be angry.

"Pikachu is the cutest Pokémon, though. We can agree on that, right?" I'm holding up a stuffed animal in front of Bryan, who is quite partial to my plushy problem.

He taps a finger along his jawline before reaching behind him. "Have you seen Evee? She seems much more up your alley." He brings up a small, fluffy brown fox-dog creature of sorts, melting my insides.

"What is she?" I take her from his hands, hauling her under my arm next to Detective Pikachu. I am so, so too old for this. I blame my cast member discount for heightening my obsession.

"You're going to get her?" Bryan laughs, strolling along the rest of the store.

"I mean, I might." I shrug, holding the dolls tight against me. So soft, so cute!

"That's right," he snaps his fingers, much more intrigued by the action figurines behind glass cases than any of the kawaii plushies. "I think Devin mentioned something about you liking stuffed animals."

My heart lurches at the sound of his name, who Bryan talks about so openly without warning. "He did?" I croak, wishing my voice weren't so fragile and obvious.

"Maybe," he shrugs casually, throwing me a small, knowing smirk. He doesn't know much, though.

"That's funny," I say, but there's nothing funny about it at all. "Have you spoken to him while he's been in California?" I ask, curiosity getting the best of me. It's easy for Devin to feel worlds away; here in this Japanese store in the middle of Florida, it's easy to think that the world is so small.

"Not much beyond begging him to send me our rent money," Bryan snorts, eyeing a particular Goku figurine. "Should have asked you to get the message across."

"He's busy, I'm sure." I roll my eyes. "He hasn't spoken to me, either."

Bryan opens his mouth to speak, but then quickly shuts it.

"What?" I challenge him, bracing myself for whatever brutality he has to offer.

"I'm just not surprised, is all."

My heart sinks.

"What does that mean?" My arms fold over my stomach.

"Just that you broke his heart. Why would he want to speak to you after that?" Bryan leans away from the glass, making a split decision to leave the action figure behind. I lose momentum at the same time, dropping the Evee in a nearby Totoro pile. I guess I don't need it anymore. Or deserve it.

I shuffle my feet. "Did he say something to you?" I feel my cheeks flushing with embarrassment.

"No, but I have eyes and ears like the rest of ya'll." His southern accent makes a rare appearance, and while my stomach is in a jumble of knots, I feel honored to have witnessed it.

We wander the rest of the store quietly, him checking out samurai swords and I finding interest in Japanese hair sticks. As we contemplate what next to hand our paychecks over to, I decide that I haven't let Bryan play an active part in my story at my own loss. His candor is fresh, needed, and surprisingly, not overwhelming. If only I'd been able to see that sooner. It's no wonder that Bethany keeps him around and Devin agrees to room with him. He's actually pretty cool, whereas I am *not*.

"How do you feel about sake?" I ask when we're both paying for an assortment of snacks and drinks to take back to our apartments for rainy days.

"The more the better," he jokes, brightening my mood.

I bump his shoulder. "Let's get some. My treat."

At the outdoor sake bar, Bryan is in awe of the fact that I don't have a sake of preference, insisting that as a result we each order a sake flight, so that I may better sophisticate my taste buds. As I go along tasting (and gagging) through the flight, it becomes increasingly apparent that I will continue to have no preference.

"Don't be mad at me, but I can almost swear these all taste the same." I wince as the warm liquid glides down my throat in a taste that's closer to rubbing alcohol from hell than anything else.

"You are tragic." Bryan tsks, excusing himself to run back to the bar and grab something else. I let him go, quietly content to at least be entertained if not anything else.

By now, the calls from Bethany and Anaya have subsided, as the girls have most likely come to terms with the fact that they have no choice but to spend the rest of the night together while Bryan and I go on enjoying our liquor. Anaya has uncharacteristically sent a message into our trio group chat that has sparingly been used since our fallout, a small "thank you" standing alone in text. Unsure as to whether she's talking to me or Bethany, I reply with a thumbs up, hoping that in some parallel dimension, my plan has worked.

I smile to myself, optimistic at heart as Bryan returns with what appears to be a small drink sample.

"Try this," he holds the drink out for me. "It's not hot, and it won't make you gag. Promise."

Carefully taking the drink in one hand while balancing my phone in the other, I grimace. "I'm trusting you, Bryan."

Upon taking a small sip, I find that Bryan is right. Whatever explosion of flavor happening in my mouth is a million times better than hot sake and has the chops to get me the buzz I want in this current state of mind. "What is this?" I grin.

"Plum wine," he bows, making me laugh. While he's off guard, I snap a photo of the wine and his arrogance, granting him the title of Sake Connoisseur on my Instagram.

"I'll give it to you, this is probably all I'll ever drink here." I boast, savoring the small cup while it lasts and also dreading having to finish my other sake samples.

"That's alright. You can save the sake for Devin and me." He winks and just on time, my phone shakes.

What, who?!?!? Sorry, I've been swamped over here. Can I call you?

"Speak of the devil." I huff, setting the wine down and responding.

"Uh oh. What he do?" Bryan asks credulously.

Can't. Out with Bryan.

I type back, smugly thinking that it might make him jealous. Have fun! He replies jet quick, sending me deflating.

"What would you do in my place, Bryan?" I ask instead, the hot sake loosening my gut.

"I'm gonna need a bit more than that, Abigail." He leans against the high top, eager as anyone else to know the real story.

"I want to be with him, but I don't know how I feel about this part-time stuff. He could end up living in California, forever. And I guess I just always saw myself here." I shrug, knowing I'm not opposed to moving somewhere else if it was for the sake of Disney, but also knowing a man is not a justifiable reason to pick up and go. "This is home for me...for all of us, I think."

Bryan nods his head sympathetically. "It's indefinite, so I know that can be scary, but I also know that Devin loves it here. He loves Florida, and he loves our crazy friends. He wouldn't leave that for just anything, and honestly, I don't know that he'd leave it for long."

"I can't rely on that, can I, though?" I say, knowing I owe it to myself to put my own dreams and ambitions first. He is quiet. "So, again, I guess what I'm asking is this: what would you do if the person you've been waiting for was leaving indefinitely? Would you wait? Would you let things go?"

"It's all or nothing for you, isn't it, huh?" Bryan grunts, observatory. "I guess it depends. If I really saw myself with that person, then why end something I think could be great?"

"I don't know." I shrug.

"Don't all the best love stories entail some waiting? *The Princess Bride*? *The Notebook*?" He's right, for me it is all or nothing. I want all of Devin or none of him, and I'm not sure that's fair for either of us. Am I being selfish? Or trying to guard my heart?

"Brownie points for those examples, Bryan. You also missed *When Harry Met Sally*." I laugh tiredly.

"I got my point across, though." He reaches over, downing one of my sakes. Not that I mind. "The real question, though, is what do you *want*?"

"That's a silly question." I swallow. "It's not that simple."

"It's not that simple only because you don't want it to be, Abigail, and *that's* what the problem is."

Nineteen

"How was your night?" Bethany pegs me when I stroll back into the apartment a few hours later, busting her sipping on a cup of hot chocolate.

"Where's mine?" I point before she directs me towards the kitchen. "Did you guys have fun?"

I watch her while I serve myself a cup from the pot, garnishing it with marshmallows and sprinkles. At first I think she may comment on me avoiding her question, but instead she tilts her head and smiles.

"Not at first, but we got around to it."

I nod happily. "I'm glad because I had little else up my sleeve."

"Have you listened to your voicemail?" Bethany grits her teeth.

"Deleted it all." I raise my brows, coming around to join her on the couch. She emits a sigh.

"We weren't very happy with you when we did those," she admits and we both laugh.

"Did you know Bryan is the king of all sake tasting?" I inquire, smirking behind my cup.

Bethany smiles shyly. "I wouldn't call him that, but yes, he's a fan of Japanese alcohol."

Just then, Anaya storms in, jumping onto the couch and pulling me into a hug.

"Abby! We missed you tonight. Did Bryan bore you to death?" She jabs me in the shoulder and I snort.

"He was great. Knew I was down, offered some sound advice."

"Well, share, hello!" Anaya groans and so I do, detailing the night among topic of inevitable discussion: Devin.

"Well, he's right," Bethany pulls up her legs beneath her. "What do you want?"

"In a perfect world? Or, you know, this one?" Sarcasm drips from my mouth and she flicks her tongue out at me. Everyone around me seems to think that this can be so simple, but they've failed to consider all the technicalities.

"Doesn't matter which one. If you want the man, go get 'em." Anaya replies briskly, releasing a snort a few moments later. "Can you believe this man is still messaging me, Beth? Asking what presets I use to get my photos!"

"Ahhh, give me that!" Bethany flings across the couch, nabbing Anaya's phone. "Who needs a dating app when you have Instagram?"

"Uhhh, what is going on?" A timid laugh escapes me, causing Anaya to groan.

"This follower has been messaging me all day, saying he likes my content and that he's a local photographer who also loves Disney, yada yada. Either way, Bethany has been responding to most of the messages." She flicks her hand indifferently, but now I want to know the gory details. Bethany is more than compliant, guiding me through an extreme background check.

"Oh my gosh!" I scream, counting over the recent exchanges after interrogating his profile. "He's cute *and* he's asking if you're free soon!" Bethany and I share a victory dance.

"Don't do it!" Anaya attempts to intercept us, but we're all practiced in the art of meddling.

"Too late, I've invited him out for New Years!" Bethany raises the phone above her head, tossing it in Anaya's direction with satisfaction. Anaya's face falls, dreading whatever mess we've just created.

"I hate you both." She says weakly. I smile, anyways. No, she doesn't. We spend the rest of the night recounting events throughout our days, boys, and other non-intimidating topics that make me so happy I feel like I can cry. Things might not be back to normal, but they're as close as they can possibly be.

"Devin gets back today, doesn't he?" Anaya prompts me the following morning after we've argued over which stores to shop at for our NYE getup.

"I think." I shrug, knowing that she's fairly right: he does get back today and has already asked to see me, though I have avoided responding to that particular message.

"You don't plan on even being his friend after all this, do you?" She watches me in a way that makes me think she barely recognizes me at all.

"Of course, I just—" I choke on my words, clearing my throat to buy me time to say something that might not land me in the doghouse. She doesn't wait to hear whatever lame excuse I can come up with, whipping on her heel and heading back to her room.

"We're all heading to Disney Springs later, if you're interested," she says, but when the door to her room slams, I don't exactly feel like it's an actual invitation.

I go regardless, wearing a scruffy Uniqlo t-shirt I purchased on my Disney College Program, one I should have thrown away ages ago but never have the nerve to. There's something too nostalgic about Hercules on a shirt for me to part ways with.

Emotions fester inside me as the girls and I trickle in and out of stores, more and more shopping bags trailing behind us with each visit. I try my best to steer clear of Anaya and any other judgmental commentary she might throw at me.

"You look like you're in physical pain." Bethany whispers out of her earshot when we make a snacking stop at Sprinkles mid-afternoon.

"Mmm, you might be onto something." I muse, laughing, because I know that things could be worse. Things may not turn out the way I'd like them to right now, but I'll be okay in the foreseeable future. She leaves me alone, though, wrapping me in a loose hug and trying her best to encourage me to try on new clothes and buy peculiar accessories. It's a distraction enough, and I really am feeling alright until we sit down to dinner and *they* show up.

"No sake here?" Bryan points at me, glancing over the Polite Pig menu.

"Unfortunate, isn't it?" I laugh, cringing internally when Devin pulls up a seat next to me. Bethany squeezes my hand in encouragement, but aside from that it's hard to imagine anyone else is here with us. "Hi." I breathe as a way of greeting without looking up from my own menu, though it must be weak and unconvincing.

"Gone a week and that's all I get? Shucks, I guess I should try a month next time," Devin jokes, but when I muster the courage to look up, his eyes are tired and his shoulders are slouched, palms laced before him on the dining table. My first instinct is to ask if he's alright, but I don't think I want the answer to that, not really.

"I'm sorry," I whisper, clearing my throat and cranking up a smile, convinced if I mimic the action eventually the emotions will wipe off on me. "How was this week?"

He shrugs his shoulders, slow and unattached. "Lots of basic shadowing, stuff that you would probably call me a nerd for telling you about."

"Oh, come on, you know I enjoy hearing it." I blurt and his mouth kicks up at the corner just slightly.

"Maybe next time," he looks up, making like he's never been in this restaurant before, taking in the sights and the sounds. Maybe with a mind like his, every time is the first time. What a beautiful thing. "How have the boats been running without me?"

"They haven't. Don't you know? The ride can't open without you there to direct everything, oh Nerd King." I roll my eyes and he knees me under the table.

"Go easy on me, will you? I've been without your harassment for some time now. You've got to ease me into it." He's laughing now, the sound of it sweet in my ears.

"That would eliminate all the fun, Dev." I tsk.

"I've missed this." His voice betrays his emotions, telling me this week has been just as hard for him as it has for me. In some other universe, I'd know how to end this in a way that works for everyone, but in this reality, I'm just Abigail, and just Abigail won't cut it.

"What?" I say, despite dreading the answer. The lights in the establishment have dimmed just a tad, reminding me too much of Ballast Point and a time when there was a potential for too many things.

"You, this, us." His cheeks flush a deep red under his worn skin, causing my fingertips to itch. I didn't think seeing him again would be this painful but it's quickly proving now to be unbearable.

"Sorry." I say simply and then let dinner resume without any other complicated interactions with the boy who's meant so much to me these last few years. Someone who has orbited at the center of my galaxy, so carelessly well-placed and now the total opposite.

Bryan tells everyone about our time together in Japan and that we'll be back very soon for round two over in Italy, where he will teach me the delicacies of their alcohol, which I'm pretty sure is just wine, but I'd hate to steal his thunder after finding out that I really do enjoy his presence.

"You know, he really isn't that bad. I see why you guys are friends, now." I give a lame attempt at keeping the peace when Anaya launches into telling everyone about her new blog and Instagram platform. She's ticked me off too much for me to want to listen, and I still have what Bryan told me stuck in my head.

"Does this mean you'll actually want to come around my apartment now?" He elbows me. A small stab of guilt hits me when I think of all the times I offered to invite him over instead of actually going to his house, all because I didn't take too well to Bryan. I see now that he's just as helpless as the rest of us. How strange the dynamic between the five of us is.

My lack of an answer is enough for him. I try to ignore the sigh he makes under his breath, knowing that if I look at him too long, parts of me I didn't know could feel would be set aflame. Is Bryan right? Am I wrong for wanting everything or nothing at all?

"Hey, Dev? Did Abigail ever tell you who came by the ride?" He speaks now, drawing me out of my stupor.

"I didn't," I shake my head, smirking in his direction. Bethany claps her hands together, laughing.

"I've never seen her so surprised!" She laughs. "Tell him!"

"Okay, well," I tilt my head. "Jessica and I were on Fastpass duty and then..." I go on, detailing every moment as if it had happened minutes earlier. I'll probably be going on about it forever and that's fine. It was great.

"So, *that's* your type." Bryan adds once I've wrapped up the great tale. Everyone howls with laughter, glad to be together once more, and my heart lifts if just a little, the normalcy I've been wanting finally back. It goes on that way, everyone around me talking, and I just relax into the intimacy of it all, forgetting everything that's proceeded us this last month.

When it's time to part ways, the boys speak of wandering the Springs a bit more but we've had enough.

"See you tomorrow," Bryan hugs me. "Drinks in Italy." He gives an extra squeeze and I nod gladly.

"I'll need it." My eyes cross jokingly and I move onto Devin.

"Bye, Abigail," he hugs me, unwilling to cross a certain line that we've tiptoed around at this point.

"Bye, Dev." I step away and then we're leaving.

No, "see you tomorrow." No, "soon." "Later."

Nothing.

And I can't have that. I can't.

"Wait," I touch Bethany's arm before turning around.

"Devin!" I yell through the crowd, making my way back to him, now maybe twenty feet away.

"Yeah?" He laughs uncertainly, turning over his shoulder and seeing me.

"Bye." I catapult myself into his arms, squeezing him like it may be the last time I see him. And, really, it might. I don't know when he's leaving. I haven't asked and I don't think I will.

He relaxes into my hold, his head up against my hair. "Bye, Abigail." He laughs sadly, but Bryan is watching us over his shoulder with a smug look on his face, arms crossed in apparent waiting.

"Yeah, okay." I nod, slowly stepping out of the embrace and consequently wishing I didn't have to.

"Wait, don't go yet." Devin throws a hand over his face, reaching with his other into his pocket.

"Yes!" Bryan cheers from behind him, jumping on his heels and covering his mouth with his fist.

"I wanted to give this to you, but I couldn't find the right time." He fishes out a tiny brown paper gift box. "Sorry that it took a little longer. I hope you like it."

"Oh, thanks." I smile timidly, but he can barely look at me. Then I leave without opening the gift, without reiterating my goodbye, without anything.

It's when I'm sitting in the car, wondering if I've made the right choice to go without any clarification, running my fingertips over the small, yet unopened gift that Anaya chooses to speak up from behind the wheel.

"You know, Abigail. I really don't get you. After everything you two have been through?" She drums her fingers against the steering wheel. My head whips up in shock.

We're at a stop, minutes away from the apartment, from me being able to muster the courage to open the gift, but she can't wait.

I don't know what to say, can't speak. Bethany is just as silent behind me.

"After he's been there for you through—"

"You know," I break through her voice, calmly as I can. "You have a lot of nerve questioning my life choices right now, Anaya."

"What?" She snaps, fueling my rage. The light turns green, but she makes no move to inch the car forward.

I take a deep breath. "Everything that happened between us all was *your* fault, and I am so, so angry at you for dragging me into this. I've tried for a long time not to blame you, but I am sick of being the nice guy. So before you decide to judge my life choices, why don't you take a second to consider yours?"

She's quiet for a moment, lets the car start to roll and slowly accelerates.

"I'm sorry," she says once we've pulled into our parking lot.

"It's fine, I'm not here to start another argument, but I could really do without the hate. You have no idea how hard this is for me right now, I don't need any extra grief. I'll do what I think is right for me." I hold a palm up as she tries to come toward me, hoping it'll keep her away. Bethany beats her to it, though, and before I know it, I'm wrapped in a hugging sandwich between the both of them.

I'll do what I think is right for me.

What's right, though?

I've spent at least two hours debating when I should open the gift, if I should do it while the girls are there, alone, or if I should really do it at all. Nothing feels just right, though, and I finally decide I should just woman up and open it at my earliest convenience, which is technically now.

The Kraft paper is tough under my fingers as I tear at the wrapping, revealing a small pink box. My hands still on the lid, hopeful and uncertain at what I'll find. A second of courage reveals that I can, in fact, lift the lid and place it to the side.

Holding my breath, I open my eyes and peek inside.

A small, involuntary gasp escapes me as I lift the priceless antique from the box.

Devin has gifted me a small compass that appears to be functioning, no doubt in thanks to his handy engineering skills. It's a mix of golds and silvers, rusted coppers and metallic burns. Upon further inspection, it dawns on me that there are bits and pieces of melted metal that I gifted him on Christmas warped into the glass. I can't imagine the time and effort it took to find the appropriate pieces and meld them together to create the masterpiece. The metallic work of art is adorned with a wooden backing, where two words have been carved into the finishing.

Love, Devin

The girls find me sometime later, when I've been lying in my bed with the compass clutched so tightly in my palm that it's slick against my hand. They don't ask me about how I feel, or what they can do. Instead, they lie down on either sides of me, shut off the light and let me cry without question.

It's the next best thing.

Twenty

"This really is beautiful," Bethany wakes me the next morning, rubbing her fingers over the glass.

"It is, isn't it?" I snuggle against the pillow, glad to be awake and out of the persistent nightmares that kept me restless all night.

"Can I see?" Anaya stirs beside me, lifting a grabby hand for the device.

"Be careful with it," I whisper, my heart thumping at the thought of anything happening to it.

"*A and D*," Anaya swoons. "This is so romantic."

"Where does it say that?" I sit up, sure I couldn't have missed any single detail of the most magical gift I've ever received in the history of all time.

"Right here," she points into the glass, both Bethany and I leaning in eagerly.

Bethany claps a hand over her mouth. "He replaced north with your initials."

"What?" I take the compass from Anaya, scrutinizing where he's removed the north face and instead scribbled his initial plus mine. "Wow." My heart lurches.

"Have you thanked him?" Bethany tries to distract me, but I'm too busy thinking about how sometimes, most times, he really is my north.

Between all the adversities, he has always been my constant, my reassurance, my support...my north.

Rather than respond, I pick up my phone and dial his number.

"Hello?" He answers on the first ring, voice laced with exhaustion and uncertainty.

"Still sleeping?" I laugh, biting my lip.

"No, no," he assures me.

"I just opened your gift." I say, but as I speak, I can hear Bryan in the back, calling out to him, asking a question.

"Hey, sorry, Abby, I have to go, but I'll call you back, okay?" He's quick to go before I can say anything else, and then any sudden encouragement I'd felt moments ago diminishes.

"Well, that went well." Anaya nods bashfully, but Bethany and I laugh. I still have my girls, who are just as much my north, and that is such a great feeling.

"C'mon. No moping today. New year, new you, boo." Bethany wags a sassy finger. We laugh even more.

"I know we're dressing to party, but I have to say, something tells me this dress is not going to look this good in five hours, no less in twelve." I sputter in the heat, dawning a short, though heavy, glittering party dress to Epcot. If anything, I'm glad I opted for some cute flats. The afternoon sun is no joke.

"Please," Bethany waves her hand as if she can care less. "No one will be paying attention past sundown, and you know that."

"Point taken." I note, knowing that not many will be coherent past that point.

Once a year, EPCOT becomes a place of ultimate, unadulterated mayhem. That day, for many like us, is New Year's Eve. Any cast member who is not working, looking to get laid, or just plain looking for a good time shows up here, which will explain why not too soon after opening, the park reaches capacity. That might sound like hell to sane people, but for us, well, it spells for a wild party come late afternoon.

"I, for one, do not care what you're wearing now and won't later." Jessica jokes, having taken me up on the offer to join us tonight. She's awarded a laugh from us all.

"See? Nothing to worry about!" Bethany pats my back.

Anaya is too busy talking with all her other park friends to notice us, and we huddle into our own corner, enjoying the scent of Italian pizza behind us and talking future plans and work schedules. While I'm having a great time, I can't help but wonder why Devin hasn't called me back or if he plans to. When Bryan arrives soon after, most of my questions are put to rest.

"This is Jessica, she was much cooler than Abby when I came around their location the other day, FYI." Bethany introduces them and Bryan puffs his chest.

"Why do we not have any famous people come through the water parks, man? It's hot." He lifts his hands in dismay, and while the girls go on to ask him questions about how cutthroat it really is being a lifeguard, I shuffle on my feet, eager to ask where the pea to his pod could possibly be, but just as I work up the nerve, flashing lights engulf the pavilion and lasers accompany the oncoming sound to techno.

Everyone cheers, falling easily into the beating pulse of music, quickly finding rhythm that works. I join in, but my heart is somewhere off in the distance.

We dance for some time, longer than I thought I could in my current state, and once I'm sweating and laughing, jumping amongst people I've never met, Bryan pulls me aside.

"Your heart isn't in this," he observes, twirling me the way Devin once did not so long ago.

"Where is he?" I ask, skipping formalities.

"I don't know," he shrugs, disappointment evident. In Devin or me, I don't know. I nod my head then, taking it as a sign to exit, and filter my way through the crowd all the way to the pizza stand. If nothing else can cure a broken heart, I can rely on pizza to do some good.

I order a pepperoni slice easy enough, basking in the salty warmth when the cheese touches my tongue, soothing the more shallow parts of my being and providing me momentary comfort. The few moments alone are nice enough, but they prove to be short lived when the rest of our small group makes their way towards me, eyes hungry with want at the sight of my miniature feast.

"Get your own." I turn my back to them before they can get too close, a small hiss in my voice.

"How's about another sake tasting, huh?" A hand drops on my shoulder. I shrug.

"I have nothing better to do."

A short, though sweat-slick, walk to Japan lands us in the center of a silent disco, where guests are head bopping to whatever music is playing on their headphones.

"It's so quiet." Bethany whispers out the side of her mouth, tiptoeing around the crowd as not to disturb them.

"I want to try this out." Jessica stops, pulling up her phone and following the directions to access the exclusive playlist. Bethany and Anaya glance at each other questioningly, but slowly follow suit.

"I'll pass." I say to Bryan, who nods his head thankfully. The crowd cheers then, jumping with vigor and starting to recite the lyrics to "Another One Bites the Dust" as we wait in line for our drinks.

After ordering, he sneaks a glance at me moving my feet to the beat before lifting his phone to his ear and waiting. A few moments pass and then he releases a sigh, pocketing his device.

"It actually seems pretty cool." I watch the crowd, looking for the girls. When I find them, they're laughing and spinning, singing and twisting with glowing headphones pulsing against their ears.

"How are you holding up?" Bryan asks, drinking his sake slow beside me. How anyone could like anything like that is beyond me. I'll stick to my plum wine, please and thank you.

"Alright," I shrug. "I always have tomorrow." Mid sip, Bryan's face pales behind the flashing disco lights. "What?" I ask, a sinking feeling that's become all familiar to me hitting all at once.

"He leaves tomorrow, Abigail." Bryan drops his glass, pushing it away from himself with a puckered face.

"What?" I'm not comprehending much, but I feel ice cold water slicing through my body. At any moment I might fall. "Why would he come back for two nights?"

Bryan laughs gruffly. "Why do you think?"

My eyes sting, any feeling of hope I might have had dissipating in an instant. Without knowing what I'm up to, I'm dialing him in a moment's notice only to be sent straight to voicemail. "No." I run a defeated palm over my face.

"Sorry." Bryan tries to pat my hand but I snake out of his reach.

"Why come back to disappear?" I shake my head, disbelieving.

"He was hoping if he came back, you'd change your mind, but then after yesterday, he was sure you were done. He gave you the gift, and I don't know. Seems to me like he's come to terms with it all."

My gut splits in half. Gone. Gone tomorrow. Gone for good. Without a goodbye.

"Alright, thanks, Bryan. I'll see you later, okay?" I raise my glass in parting, taking it with me as my last bit of company.

Just as I go, trekking up the steps to the hidden koi ponds of Japan, a teleprompter notifies the crowds that there's only ten minutes till midnight. Everyone cheers.

"If I could go back, what would I do differently?" I ask the koi, knowing that they will be far from helpful and the only person I can rely on at this point is myself. Realistically, I think I wouldn't change much, aside from the mentality that a little change to my world can bring about something horrible. After all, just because someone is leaving doesn't mean it's final. Maybe I've been emotionally selfish to not want to deal with those changes, and maybe, just maybe, I'll be missing out on something grand if I choose to think that way. And, really, while this thinking is safe, I don't exactly *want* to keep thinking this way. It might just be what's keeping me from a better role here at Disney, an unexpected route, new friends, love...

A small smile lights up my face, reflecting in the water below me where koi are coming up for food, hoping to get a bite from me. My phone rings just then.

"Hello?" I answer without checking who it might be.

"Get back here! There's only a few minutes till midnight!" Bethany or Anaya, or maybe both, are shouting into the receiver.

"Yeah, okay." I laugh, ready for whatever comes next.

They reveal themselves a few steps down and across the pond over by the Mitsukoshi store, jumping up and down, arms flailing to catch my attention.

"There you are!" Bethany grins wildly, and I don't know if she's wasted or just in a great mood.

"Here I am!" I echo, leaning against the bubble window behind us. "Not sure this is a great firework viewing location, though."

"It is!" Anaya persists, leaving her Instagram passé and taking my hands, swinging me so that she's up against the window and I'm facing just opposite, the indoor lights glowing behind her frame.

"Now it really isn't." My eyes roll involuntarily. Today has been a whirlwind, and I'd at least like to experience something worthwhile before the end of the night.

"Yes. It. *Is*." Bethany snaps her fingers by my eyes, pointing behind her.

"Do you not want to watch the fireworks? We can go inside." I speak slowly, agitation seeping into my voice.

"Come on, Abigail. Don't be dense!" Anaya moves to the side. They both viciously begin pointing inside.

"What are you doing?" I chuckle at the sheer idiocrasy of their movements. Then I see it. "Oh!" I gasp, watching a very specific guy pick up a very cute stuffed animal.

"Dev!" I pound on the glass, reminiscent of Darla in *Finding Nemo*. It's not intentional, but it's New Years, you know? A few knocks get me nothing, and he continues to aimlessly wander around the anime section, though he does not drop the little caramel dog-fox. Desperate, Bethany and Anaya join in, banging as if their life depends on it. Note to self: Disney has invested in hurricane-resistant windows. Smart of them.

A deep laugh behind me tells me that Bryan is watching the entire exchange, and just as I'm about to lose hope, he looks over his shoulder, eyes fixed on nothing in particular.

"Devin, hello!" We all shout, and finally, his eyes widen, realization dawning on him. His cheeks redden and he lifts the child's toy in a small wave.

"Come here," I beckon, flicking my wrists, the girls encouraging him to do the same.

He looks around helplessly and then finally nods.

"Taking too long." I grumble, pushing past the masses and making my way for the side entrance. Just as I'm about to go in, he comes out and we collide.

"'Hey," he says, voice far from cool.

"Hi," I sigh, glad to see him, sad that it's taken this long, and thankful that I have this chance. "I tried to call you, but I..."

"My phone's been out of battery, so if you..."

Our voices crash and we each come to a halt, laughing.

"I loved your gift, Dev. It's beautiful." I take his hand, squeezing. "Thank you." A countdown is starting behind us, but everything outside of this moment is irrelevant, a small dent on my existence, whereas whatever comes next is forever.

"Look, Abigail. I'm sorry if I made you feel bad. I understand that you might not want to wait for me, or have to deal with the strain of long distance. I just wish that we could still be friends without all of this bearing down on us. At the end of the day, it's always been me and you, and if you don't want it to be that way romantically, I'm fine with it. Just having you in my life is a gift enough, and I can't imagine axing you out of mine completely. I hate it, I can't stand the thought of it." His face looks so torn, voice gruff with desperation, and I want nothing more than to change that, and I know that in just a few seconds, I will.

"I don't *want* to be your friend, Devin." I say, and the way his eyes drop in defeat tells me he thinks that I've finally gone through with the possibility of cutting him off completely, a clean break. "The truth is...the thought of being here without you hurts, but not as much as the thought of having you out of my life for good, and definitely not as much as just being your friend." I laugh, the words feeling so foreign to me. Devin's always been the one chasing me, and I never thought the roles would be reserved, but I guess I do owe him the favor. He's been pretty damn great.

"Wait..." his expression goes through a range of emotions, sadness, elation, perplexity. "Are you saying what I think you're saying?"

"Ya know," I put my thumb to my lip, feinting really considering it. "I think I might be." The noise level considerably heightens behind us when I move his palm to my chest, cradling it against my heart. He nearly shakes with giddiness.

"So, you want to do this? You really want to do this? I won't be gone long, I'll come visit, but, I mean, you'll have to—" he moves closer, itching with uncertainty.

"You sure do have a lot of questions for an engineering intern." I tease, moving his arm behind me and winking. He opens his mouth to speak, but I shush him with a kiss just as the fireworks erupt behind us, turning the back of my eyelids blue and pink and green.

Everything is going to be just fine...more than fine, even.

The thought comes naturally as my toes curl at the way he takes my face in his hands and deepens the kiss. Unfortunately, it just so happens to be short lived.

"Happy New Year!" We're attacked all at once by a bundle of arms and leggings wrapping us in warm greetings.

Devin and I exchange a pointed look, disappointed at yet again another moment being sabotaged. At least we got to the good part this time, though. "Anaya!" We say, laughing madly at the jinx.

"What!" She slaps my arm, but then the rest of our friends are there, blowing horns and wishing us well.

"You know," Devin tugs on my hand when we finally have enough space to breathe without rubbing up on someone else's body. "I was told you were a big fan of a Pokémon plush back in there."

"Oh, I am." I wrap my arms around his neck, my body humming with joy at being near him. It may be for the last time in a while, but I know it'll be enough for us. Something like this doesn't just disappear, and I really, truly hope it doesn't.

"So," his nose brushes mine. "Did you want me to go back and get that or?" He leaves the question opened-ended, making me laugh. I've missed his careless charm, always eager to find ways to amuse me.

"Yeah, I do." I nod all businesslike so he knows I take my collecting seriously, but just as he's about to untangle himself from me, I pull him in for a kiss. One he'll remember me by come tomorrow when he hops a plane to his dream, and one for me while I keep up the good work back here, consciously developing mine.

For the next few minutes or so, the toy will have to wait.

Epilogue

I swish the green dress around my legs, glancing over my shoulder at the cameraman.

"That's a really good one." He smiles, lifting from his kneed position in the dirt, coming over to show me what he's captured.

While I'm still not keen on being the center of attention, Anaya insists that I chronicle all of my travels to add to the blog. It is in good taste for the editor-in-chief to occasionally show her face, after all. Besides, Disney can't always be the center of attention, can it?

"I dare say that you're biased." I roll my eyes. I'm no model and he's no real photographer, but I'm sure Anaya can figure out something that works for her. Besides, her new motto is about broadcasting the good, the bad, and the ugly...the real. While I still think the internet is mostly jaded, she's made it her mission to be as genuine as possible on her new platform, and so far, that's going great. Bethany makes time to develop the look of the blog when she can, but between being newly appointed as a trainer to new hires, it's not always feasible. As for me, I've gone part-time for the company, picking up shifts when I find extra time but mainly focusing on getting my Master's degree in Hospitality. Hopefully, with some network-ing I'll be able to land a teaching position at Disney University once I'm done. A girl can dream.

"I don't see how I couldn't be," Devin winks. "You're quite the woman." It's been eight months since Devin has taken off to California, and in two weeks, he'll be eligible to be hired as a full-time Imagineer. While he loves all the Mexican street food that's readily available at a moment's notice in L.A., he'll also be eligible to transfer back to Orlando soon and can't wait to get back. He says it's because he misses living with Bryan, but I know better.

"Thanks, loser." I scuffle the toe of my boot, leaning into his arms. The weather in Texas isn't as brutal as Florida's in August, but the desert-like surrounding would have you thinking otherwise. The Alamo is pretty amazing, but without the context, it may just look like a small mound of rock. Luckily, I'm stuck with a great guide.

Yesterday, we stayed with his parents in Austin, where he broke the news that he had an early Christmas present for me. Handing me a printed airline confirmation page, he revealed come New Year's, we'll be standing under the Eiffel tour, embracing the Parisan city lights. It all feels like a dream, and yet, just under a year ago, none of it seemed possible.

"I can't believe it's been eight months." I muse now, reflecting on everything we've had to battle since then. Short weekend trips back and forth, oddly-timed Skype calls, missed texts, silent holidays, but it hasn't been all that bad, not with knowing everything that's waiting for us.

"Are you happy?" Devin asks, refraining from mentioning that soon it'll be over. He's one of the best new engineering assets the company has, and they've seen that. He'll easily transfer in the next few months and then everything will change again. For better or worse? Unknown. While this has been an adjustment, it's allowed me so much room to grow, so much time to mend and strengthen friendships, encouragement to discover, explore, and push myself in ways I didn't think I could before. All thanks to my friends, but more so, all thanks to me for accepting the change, the opportunity to bloom.

A slow smile creeps up on me, the setting of the sun shining on our unsuspecting faces. A laugh escapes us as we reach up to shield our eyes from the glare.

"More than happy."

Interview with the Author

What inspired you to write this novel?

For me, so much of this novel came from the feeling I got working for the Walt Disney, and how everything felt as if it was crashing around me when, after my Disney College Program in 2014, I decided it was time for me to head home. There were so many more things I wish I had done while working for the Mouse; so many people I wish I'd spent more time with, others I wish I was honest with, and those I still to this day I wish I could bottle up and keep with me always. I originally thought that my first novel, *Finding Fantasyland*, was an ode to my DCP, but it wasn't until I wrote this novel that I truly felt I was letting go of everything that took place during my time in Orlando and that I could move on from that. So, really, I guess what I'm trying to say, is this is the love song to a time that now almost feels like a dream.

How did this novel compare to your own time working for Walt Disney World?

If I'm being quite honest, a lot of what goes on in *Awaking Adventureland* is not all too farfetched from my own experience. Disney hookup culture is real, cast members are people, your DCP friends almost always become family.

What was your favorite/least favorite thing about working with the company?

I think the best part about working for the company was the people. Everyone is so eager to be kind and make new friends, which made it seamless to transition into living in a new city with a bunch of strangers. It's also great to be a part of

something you know so many people care about. Bonding over
Disney culture is always fun. The worst thing would have to
be the pay and how quickly some people come and go, whether
onto new work locations or just back home.

**Is it safe to say, then, that Abigail's worst nightmare hap-
pened to you? Everyone left?**

Absolutely, but I think Abigail still has a lot to learn from life,
even post *Awaking Adventureland*. Most of my Disney cast
member friends left after their program or worked another year
or two in Orlando before heading back home. It isn't terrible,
though, we've all kept in touch and have seen each other a few
times since then. Even those who I haven't quite caught up with,
I still reach out to now and then. I think what Abigail still has to
learn is that there really is life outside of Disney, even if it seems
unbelievable. That, of course, doesn't mean I'm not always considering packing up and going back to where it all began.

So...did you really meet Capt.?

That's a hard no, though a few friends caught sight of him!
While working for the company, I met quite a few other
celebrities, though. Think Hansen, Sugar Ray, Smash Mouth—
mainly all of the Eat to The Beat performers, plus bigshots like
Johnny Depp, lots of football players, and a few notable Disney
Imagineers.

And how does Snoop Dogg like his chicken nuggets cooked?

Extra crispy! No – just kidding. I personally never met him,
but an old roommate of mine once brought out his meal to him
on the second floor of Pinocchio's Village Haus. She said he
was decked out in full Disney gear: Goofy hat and everything.
You'd be surprised what odd requests you hear about celebrities having when they come into the park. Some are great and
really make our work easy, others are pretty jaded.

**How did you tie all that you know into the Disney influ-
encer culture?**

Without divulging too much about this, I can say that the
online Disney community is not always the nicest or most

honest. While I'm online and see/hear most of what goes on, I've never been an Anaya. Word travels fast through the grapevine, though, and it isn't uncommon for someone to go from being the most loved influencer to the most despised overnight. What made me want to include this was the ever-growing popularity of online Disney fame and the mystery that sort of shrouds it for those outside looking in.

About the Author

Once upon a time Stephanie spent most of her days working for the Mouse. She's since gone on to become a high school English teacher. Her debut novel, *Finding Fantasyland*, was first published in 2015 and is followed by its companion novel, *Awaking Adventureland*. You can follow her @stephest21 on Twitter and @SafariStephanie on Instagram.

ABOUT THEME PARK PRESS

Theme Park Press publishes books primarily about the Disney company, its history, culture, films, animation, and theme parks, as well as theme parks in general.

Our authors include noted historians, animators, Imagineers, and experts in the theme park industry.

We also publish many books by first-time authors, with topics ranging from fiction to theme park guides.

And we're always looking for new talent. If you'd like to write for us, or if you're interested in the many other titles in our catalog, please visit:

www.ThemeParkPress.com

• •

Theme Park Press Newsletter

Subscribe to our free email newsletter and enjoy:

- ◆ Free book downloads and giveaways
- ◆ Access to excerpts from our many books
- ◆ Announcements of forthcoming releases
- ◆ Exclusive additional content and chapters
- ◆ And more good stuff available nowhere else

To subscribe, visit www.ThemeParkPress.com, or send email to newsletter@themeparkpress.com.

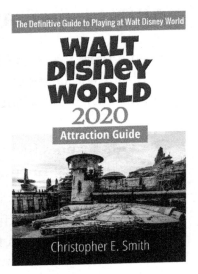

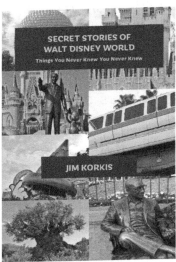

Read more about these books
and our many other titles at:
www.ThemeParkPress.com